BIG CAT MAGIC

HEART OF THE COUGAR
BOOK 11

TERRY SPEAR

PUBLISHED BY: Terry Spear

Book Cover Art by Leigh Cover Designs

Copyright ©2022 Terry Spear

Ebook ISBN: 978-1-63311-086-1

Print ISBN: 978-1-63311-087-8

Discover more about Terry Spear at: www.terryspear.com

SYNOPSIS FOR BIG CAT MAGIC

Where magic becomes reality.

Rosalie Squire needs a place to raise her teenage step-brother, Eric, away from civilized towns. She's a cougar, he's a snow leopard and a handful. She and her brother inherit a mansion that's been abandoned for years. Inheritances from their parents and their dad's cousin, the income from writing her popular spell caster novels, and sales from Eric's fantasy artwork, *when* she can get him to focus on it, gives them the financial backing to manage the estate. Wild Ridge Mansion is near Yuma Town, is truly worthy of being called a haunted house, and it's nearly Halloween!

Cougar shifter Kolby Jones is busy working on his bosses' horse ranch as a ranch hand near Yuma Town, when he swears he sees a snow leopard off in the distance. He knew he'd partied too much with the other ranch hands the night before in cele-bration of delivering a foal that day. He had too much work to do to chase phantoms of his imagination. But when he learns someone new has taken over the forsaken Wild Ridge Mansion just down the road from the Havertons' ranch, he soon discovers a whole new world of mystery, magic, and mayhem.

Thanks so much to Madeleine Gombert who loves my books and whose claim to fame is that she is my Biggest Fan Ever!! Love it! Thanks, Madeleine. You make my day!

1

"I'm going out!" Eric Squire said angrily to his stepsister, Rosalie, letting the door slam behind him on the way out of the Wild Ridge Mansion located near Yuma Town, Colorado.

The mansion looked like a castle made of stones with one tower that reached four stories high. The rest of the building was two stories tall. At one time, Rosalie's Great Uncle Max and Great Aunt Charity Squire had owned and managed it. When they died, they'd left it to an only son who was living in NYC who hadn't wanted to leave the city to manage it. He'd kept it as an investment and paid the property taxes on the mansion, but once he'd passed on, he'd left it to Rosalie's dad, his cousin. Sadly, her dad had died five years earlier—so Rosalie and her brother inherited it.

She'd worried when Eric had slammed the door, it would fall off its hinges, but it seemed sturdy enough to withstand her brother's anger. Every time she had seen the mansion when they had passed through the area on family trips, she knew it needed to be taken care of, loved like it had been at one time, and restored to its former glory. She never thought she had been related to the previous owners or that she and Eric would inherit it! She wanted to see if there were any mementos, pictures or such of the family, anywhere in the mansion.

She sighed. Her brother was fifteen, she was twenty-five, and she'd been caring for him on her own for the five years since her dad and his mother had died. Eric had been a handful for the last couple of years.

Rosalie had lost her own mother in a boating accident when she had turned five. When her surgeon father met Eric's mom, who also had been a surgeon, and fell in love with her and her two-year-old son, Rosalie had been twelve. Rosalie had adored Eric like he was her own flesh and blood brother. His mother had loved her like she was her own daughter. Rosalie had been excited to babysit her new little brother and Eric had treasured her too. Rosalie had loved her stepmother and was glad her father had found her to marry. Rosalie had thought her stepmother and brother were fascinating for being snow leopards. Before Eric was even born, his biological father had taken off for Alaska and never returned. He hadn't had family up there, just snow leopard friends, according to Eric's mother. She finally divorced him and then met Rosalie's dad while both were working at the hospital in Loveland, Colorado.

Everything had been fine between Rosalie and her brother until three years ago when he'd become a real handful. Eric had been young enough at first to abide by Rosalie's rules, but when he turned thirteen, all bets were off. They'd had so many arguments about him running as a snow leopard in Loveland, Colorado whenever he wanted, when she knew it wasn't a good idea. When they inherited Wild Ridge Mansion, he agreed to moving out there with her—with the provision he could run as a snow leopard out on their new property any time he wanted to.

She'd hoped he would at least stay at the mansion until they could receive their stuff from the moving van and get settled in a little bit.

They'd barely unpacked her SUV when Eric had stormed off, unhappy he had to live in the dusty old mansion, even though he'd agreed before that this was the best thing for them. She conceded it was a mess. All the furniture was covered in plastic, making it look spooky. At least the power had been restored, water too, but they still had an installer coming to hook up the Wi-Fi. They were far enough out, but close enough to Yuma Town that they could get internet, something both of them desperately needed for their work.

The moving van was arriving within the hour, and she glanced out the door and saw the guy arrive to hook up their internet. Yes!

She knew the huge estate was going to be a whole lot of work. But at least they could afford to update it using Eric's and her combined inheritances. He really needed a father-figure in his life to mentor him. At least she was twenty-five, or would be on Halloween, so she was like a big sister, almost a mom to him, but he wouldn't see it that way.

Twelve bedrooms, each with their own fireplaces and private bathrooms, were available that they could choose from in the formidable mansion. To attempt to appease him, she was going to let him select the one he wanted for his own first. When he ran off, she quashed that notion and looked through each of the rooms on the second floor to find the one she wanted. Man, was everything dusty.

Eric better not be seen by the movers or the internet guy while wearing his snow leopard coat. She showed the internet installation guy where she wanted the WiFi set up. Then he installed everything, and he finally left.

She was so glad that was done. She needed to remove all the bedding in her room and replace the mattress and bedding with

her own. They needed to do the same with whichever bedroom
Eric picked for his own.

Maybe, someday, she could rent out the other rooms to
guests, if she could get the place cleaned up, refurbished, and
had the time to do it. She yanked the bedcovers off the bed and
dust motes floated in the area. The mahogany bedframe was so
beautiful, she would keep it and get rid of the cheap metal frame
she'd been sleeping on for some years. The room was light and
airy with big eight-foot windows looking out on the mountains
and the gardens. The walls were pale yellow, and a beautiful fireplace with white marble and brick was situated on one wall with
bookcases on either side, painted white. She loved the big airy
casement windows and the white moldings that made the rooms
look rich in appearance. Two bedside tables and a highboy had
Queen Anne curved and carved legs, and the cedar chest at the
foot of the bed was also of mahogany.

She heard the moving truck arrive out front. Yes! She was so
glad to be able to get their kitchen items, desks for their computers, and all the rest of their household goods.

She hurried downstairs to meet the movers and began
having them move their mattresses upstairs first. She had
already paid them extra to take the mansion's mattresses they
were replacing out with them. She just picked one of the rooms
for Eric—the tower room, which was really large and had beautiful views. Knowing him, he wouldn't be happy with the choice
she'd made for him, but she figured she and he could move his
mattress again afterward, if they had to. Though it annoyed her
that he wouldn't be here to pick out his room in the first place.

The mansion was in the boonies, their property bordering a
horse ranch. Since she wrote a popular spell caster novel series
that paid the bills also, she could work anywhere. When she
could get Eric to paint his beautiful, fantasy artwork and sell it,
even paying him to make the book covers for her own books, he

had his own income. Just like her work, he could do what he loved to do out here also.

They couldn't live near other people, not when Eric needed to run as a snow leopard and get some of his unspent energy out. This way, hopefully, he wouldn't cause himself or anyone else trouble. She used to run with him and watch out for him, but he was now of the age that he wanted to run and explore on his own.

In the beginning, Eric had vehemently opposed moving to the mansion he swore had to be haunted by dozens of former residents, until she promised he could run in his fur coat any time he wanted, which was why she suspected he was testing her promise and took off in broad daylight! This place had lots of acreage, fairly close to the small town, but far enough away from civilization that they both could run as big cats safely. Then she could keep him out of trouble. At least that's what she hoped.

Once the men had finished unloading the rest of their household goods, they finally drove off. Rosalie saw her brother headed for the house, running as a snow leopard. Damn! She hoped the movers hadn't seen him through the truck's mirrors. She let out her breath, sure lecturing her brother wouldn't make a whole lot of difference. Where had he left his clothes?

He went inside the house and when she entered the home, he had shifted and was digging through his suitcase for some clothes to wear. He pulled them out and was dressing in the living room.

"We came out here to get away from people, but when we have visitors, we need to keep our wilder sides out of sight," she reminded him.

"They didn't see me." Then Eric frowned.

"You left here as a human. Where did you leave your clothes?" And why run home as a snow leopard?

He let out his breath, yanking his shirt over his head. "I saw a black bear sniffing at my clothes, so I raced back here."

"A bear?" She hadn't expected that! Here she thought it would be safer for them running out here.

"Yeah. So when the coast is clear, I have to go get them."

"I'll go with you, but we'll wait for a couple of hours until he's left the area." She sure didn't want to tangle with a bear.

"Where did you have them put my mattress?" Eric asked her, pulling on his other hiking shoe.

"In a room that hopefully you'll be happy with. If you'd been here and not run off, when I told you the moving truck was on its way, you could have picked out your room and we wouldn't have to move anything again." She ought to let him figure it out for himself since he'd been so inconsiderate to run off like that.

He scoffed. "I'm sure you picked the perfect room for me."

"I know you wanted a big room and this one is the largest room and has a view of the mountains. It's in the tower room."

Of course he was still giving her attitude and he didn't look happy about any of it.

KOLBY JONES WAS BREAKING a horse that morning on Hal and Tracey Haverton's horse ranch near Yuma Town when he looked up and he swore he saw a snow leopard running way off in the distance on that fall day. He closed his eyes and opened them, to clear his focus. There was nothing running off in the distance.

He knew he'd partied too much with the other ranch hands the night before, celebrating the successful delivery of a foal that day. He had too much work to do to chase phantoms of his imagination.

Hal came out to see how he was doing, his blond hair a little shaggier than usual, his dark brown eyes smiling. "Hey, thanks for helping to deliver the foal last night. Tracey and I sure appreciate all you do for us."

Kolby smiled. "I was just glad it all had turned out like it had."

"Well, you've taken on so many more roles here at the ranch, that we really appreciate all you do. I'm going to check on the foal." Hal took off for the stable.

Kolby had taken over Ted Weekum's bedroom at the bunkhouse, elevating his lifestyle once the ranch foreman mated a white cougar, Stella, and built their own home on the property. So naturally, Kolby had felt like top dog for the time being, in charge of the new ranch hands while Ted was away with his mate.

Hal and Tracey had taken Kolby and his brother, Ricky, in to work at the ranch, both having been turned into cougar shifters, until his brother became a deputy sheriff of Yuma Town. Kolby had thought of taking up the work Tracey had done as a special agent for the US Fish and Wildlife Service, FSWS, chasing down criminals who poached and other illegal stuff. But he loved working with the horses, teaching kids and adults to ride, living on the ranch with the other ranch hands, and working with Ted and the Havertons. He even loved playing with their quadruplets that had been out with him while jumping into a pile of leaves he'd raked up just for them, until they had to go back into the house for lunch. Speaking of which, he needed to drive in to Yuma Town and pick up the sandwiches from Fitz's Bakery and Coffee Shop for the guys.

"Hey," Ted said to him, coming out of the hay barn. "Are you still here? We're starving."

Kolby smiled, saluted him, and headed for his pickup.

2

Rosalie took Eric upstairs to the only room in the tower on the fourth floor. It was a really nice, large room, with eight-foot-tall windows that showed off views of the mountains and gardens out front and in the back of the mansion. Surrounded by low rock walls, the gardens had been neglected for years and she thought it would be fun to restore them.

He looked around at the floral-papered walls, a king-size bed, a sofa, two chairs, a desk, and cushion-covered bench. Then he went to the window and pulled back the drapes and observed the mountain view. His room also had a fireplace surrounded by marble and brickwork. Then he checked out the bathroom. It had a shower, commode, and pedestal sink all in white with a white painted cabinet for supplies situated next to the sink. He came out of the bathroom but didn't say a word.

"We inherited a lot of money from our parents and then the estate, so I figure we can put some funds into updating the parts of the mansion we'll spend the most time in. My office, your art studio—"

Eric glanced at her.

"Yes, we have so many meeting rooms downstairs that you can have your own art studio even. And I'll have my own office."

He gave her a glimmer of a smile. *Finally.*

"I want to refurbish our bedrooms, living area, kitchen, bathrooms, the den, and a library too." Neither of them really had any friends in Loveland, Colorado where they were from because they hadn't known any other big cats there. Forming close friendships with humans could lead to real trouble if they'd ever discovered what they were.

Rosalie had taken a peek in the library at one point and had discovered it was filled with books, news clippings, and photos of all the happenings about Yuma Town since its inception until Charity had died. In one article, it had stated Charity had generously set up the library so that others could borrow from her vast collection of books, and she had even ordered books that townsfolks were interested in reading. She also had a huge collection of books on gardening and woodworking.

Rosalie had realized the library was filled with a treasure trove of Yuma Town history.

"Where's your bedroom?" He still hadn't said whether he was happy with his room or not.

She hoped he wouldn't say he wanted her room. Though she wouldn't mind the tower room where she had all those views.

To keep the peace, she'd probably go along with it, but she really didn't want to have to move those heavy king size mattresses, especially when they could have had the movers set them up in the right place the first time. Then again, they wouldn't really have to change out mattresses, if he didn't mind the feel of her mattress. Hers was a little softer than his.

She led him downstairs and then down the long hall on the second-story floor to her bedroom.

"Geez, sis, did you have to put me in a room that far away? I don't play my music that loudly."

He didn't need to. With their enhanced cat hearing she heard it anyway and he never played it too loud either. He'd hurt his own ears if he did.

"I thought you felt you needed more space. Your room is huge and with all those views, it's really a beautiful room." She thought he looked a little like he was worried about being alone in this huge old place. "But we can move you into a bedroom that's closer to mine if you want."

He looked into her room and checked out the view and her bathroom. "It looks nearly the same as mine, but more...girly." She suspected he didn't want to admit he might be scared staying in a room too far away from her in the big, haunted-looking mansion.

"Right. We'll have fun making them our own bedrooms when we have time."

He grunted.

She didn't remember ever having been a sulky teenager like him. He'd been so cheerful and such a happy kid until he turned thirteen.

She wanted to get a little writing done today, but she was afraid they needed to get a lot more of their things sorted before she could really sit down and concentrate on her current book. She wished he was more enthusiastic about helping her.

"I'm hungry," he finally said.

She swore Eric was always hungry. "Okay, I haven't started to unpack our stuff in the kitchen so I was thinking we could eat out or order in."

"What restaurants do they have here?" he asked.

"They have a Jose's Mexican Restaurant and Fitz's Bakery and Coffee Shop that has soups, sandwiches, and desserts. Also the Watering Hole Bar and Grill serves pizzas, hamburgers, and fries, and an ice cream store, the Cup and Cone would be great sometime."

"Let's go to the bakery shop this time."

"Here or—"

"There. This place is so dusty."

She agreed with him there. "You can help me clean."

"I'll mow the grass."

She rolled her eyes at him. "We don't have a lawn tractor—yet." Then they left the house, got into her SUV, and headed into Yuma Town to the bakery shop.

They drove through the quaint Yuma Town, looking like a Colorado mining town with old and new buildings alike. But all the buildings were really cute—striped awnings over windows, storefronts decorated in pumpkins, autumn wreaths, and scarecrows.

The bakery was adorable, with big white windows, a pink and white-striped canvas awning out front, white chairs and tables inside, accents of honey oak throughout. White café tables were situated out under the awnings and a pink bicycle display stand with baskets on the front and back were filled with pink pumpkins and flowers.

The whole cheery bakery was decorated in fall decorations —pink pumpkins throughout, a mixture of fall flowers of orange and pink in filigree vases sitting on each of the tables. More flowers were mixed in with the pumpkins on the counters and in the window displays, and pink crystal candleholders caught the reflection of light from the window and the chandelier, making them look magical. Even the girl and boy scarecrows sitting in the window were dressed in pink plaid shirts, blue jeans wearing pink flowery patches, straw hats decorated in pink flowers in four sizes—tiny, small, medium, and large—all for sale, sitting on several mini pink quilts. A little sign on them said they were the creations of Betty Kretchen. They were the cutest things and Rosalie wanted to get a couple of the scarecrows and a quilt to decorate the mansion for the fall.

When they walked inside the shop, she and her brother not only smelled the delightful aroma of sweet treats like pumpkin spice cake, but also the delicious smells of roast beef sandwiches and French onion soup.

Three crystal chandeliers were hanging from the ceiling and white sconces were secured to pink walls. A white wood paneled counter, a pink granite countertop and cabinets all in white paneled wood separated the eating area from the kitchen and added to the fresh airy look. This place was great. Of course, Eric was frowning, and she knew he didn't like that it looked like a tearoom that she loved to go to.

"Welcome," an older woman said, curly white hair framing her heart-shaped face. She had sparkling blue eyes, and cheerful laugh lines beneath her eyes and dimples in her cheeks as she greeted them. She showed them to a table next to the window, then handed them menus. Her eyes instantly widened, but not any more so than Rosalie's and Eric's. The woman smiled broadly. "You're not from around here."

"You're a—" Rosalie didn't say what was on the tip of her tongue. She'd smelled humans dining in here also. But other cougar smells were prevalent too.

"Yep, and so are you. I'm Florence Fitzgerald. Nearly everyone calls me Mrs. Fitz and I own this place." Then she frowned at Eric. "But you're not exactly like us."

"Nope," Eric said, looking at the menu. "I'm much more exotic. Unique."

"I'll say. So are you just passing through then?" Mrs. Fitz asked them.

"We inherited Wild Ridge Mansion and just moved in there today," Rosalie said, amazed the woman was a cougar like her.

"Oh, my, well, how exciting. I've heard Max Squire was a real friendly guy, and his wife, Charity, was really sweet, though that was before my time. Charity even had a lady's book club and teatime at the mansion on a monthly basis." Then Mrs. Fitz changed subjects. "To welcome you to Yuma Town, I'd like to bring you fresh baked pastries for breakfast in the morning."

"Oh, thanks, but you don't have to do that," Rosalie said.

"Yeah, she does. We don't have anything to eat until the kitchen is ready for it," Eric said.

Rosalie gave him a scolding look. "By the way, I'm Rosalie Squire and this is my brother Eric." She wanted to tack on: who's being rude.

"Nice to meet you both."

Eric ordered the Chicken, Bacon, Ranch Melt, Chicken and Wild Rice Soup, and the Whoopie Pie for dessert. "For breakfast, I want two bear claws."

Rosalie sighed, feeling like she had to talk to him about not asking for more than just one when Mrs. Fitz was just being nice. "I'll have a Reuben, French onion soup, and a chocolate mousse for dessert. Thanks so much for the offer of pastries for breakfast. I'll have a chocolate long john."

"Good show." Mrs. Fitz retreated to the kitchen and a woman headed out to see them, bringing them ice waters.

"Hi, I'm Ava Kensington. You're an honest-to-goodness snow leopard?" She spoke low for their ears only.

"You're a cougar too?" But then Rosalie figured Ava was Mrs. Fitz's relative and working here with her.

"Oh, yeah." Ava smiled broadly. "Yuma Town is cougar run."

Rosalie's jaw dropped. "No."

Eric shook his head. "You really didn't know it, sis?"

"No, of course not. Dad never even told us we had relatives who owned the mansion," Rosalie said.

"So you inherited the old Squires' estate, Wild Ridge Mansion, then," Ava said.

"Uh, yes. It needs a lot of work I'm afraid," Rosalie admitted.

"I'll say," Eric said. "It's like a big, haunted mansion. I'm sure Dracula lives there still."

Ava laughed about Eric saying that Dracula lived there. "One thing about us here, we all help each other out." Her face suddenly brightened. "You wouldn't want to host the annual Halloween party at your estate, would you?"

"How much does it pay?" Eric immediately asked.

"We'll have to discuss it, but that old place would be perfect to host a Halloween party. You won't have to worry about decorating or preparing meals or anything. Everyone will chip in to help out. Your contribution would be the use of the facility, but I'm sure we can pay for the party to be held there also."

"I don't know," Rosalie said, thinking she didn't want a ton of strangers in their home at this point. What if they had a wild party and trashed the place?

"Oh, and believe me, everyone will clean up afterward. You won't have a thing to worry about. Just think on it. Here's my card." Ava handed her card for the shop that said she was a pastry chef.

How cool was that?

Then Mrs. Fitz came out with their soups and set them on the table. "Enjoy."

"Thanks," Rosalie said.

Eric started eating his soup.

"We had the Halloween party at the community center one year. Last year it was at the Haverton's horse ranch, which borders your property. You probably can't see the ranch houses from the mansion because there's so much land in between the two of you," Ava said. "I've got to run and get back to work in the kitchen." She smiled and hurried off.

"It would be great fun to have the party at the old mansion, but you just moved in and I'm sure you want to get to know us first a little better and get settled in more. Though the actual party won't be for another two months. So who all lives with you at the mansion?" Mrs. Fitz asked.

"Just us," Rosalie said.

"Oh, uh, all right." Mrs. Fitz sounded a little surprised to hear it.

Yeah, they'd taken over a monster of a place, just the two of them.

"Don't be surprised if many of our townspeople come out to welcome you to the area," Mrs. Fitz said.

"Okay." Rosalie was glad for the warning.

Then Mrs. Fitz nodded and saw more people coming into the shop and hurried off to greet them.

"I thought you wanted to get away from people and that's why we moved out here," Eric said.

"From humans, not our own kind."

"They're not my kind," Eric said morosely.

"They're shifters like us," Rosalie said, annoyed with her brother. Sure, they weren't snow leopards, but they still had more in common with them than humans did! And her father and his mother had loved each other, despite their differences, so get over it already! There was just no pleasing her brother of late. "It's a good thing. We'll have more friends and—"

"For you, it is. You'll meet some guy and—"

So that's what this was all about? He felt she might abandon him? His dad had, and then his mother and stepfather had died. Now all he had was Rosalie and he thought she'd leave him too?

She opened her mouth to speak when a man walked into the shop and Mrs. Fitz smiled brightly at him. "Oh, come over and meet your new neighbors, Kolby."

"Neighbors?" Kolby asked, the heavenly timbre of his voice caressing Rosalie like silk.

He was drop-dead gorgeous, blond hair highlighted by the sun, swimmingly blue eyes, tall and lean, except for his muscled arms, his face tanned, and he was wearing a Stetson. He looked like he worked and played out-of-doors a lot. He was employed at the horse ranch near their place, she bet. He couldn't be the ranch owner.

Smiling, Kolby came over to meet them, though he looked a little wary. That was until he smelled her scent and his smile broadened. But then he turned his attention to Eric and frowned. She narrowed her eyes at Kolby, not liking that he could be making her brother feel self-conscious about being a snow leopard.

"I saw you," Kolby said to Eric, still frowning.

She turned to stare hard at her brother. "He *saw* you?" What had she told Eric about avoiding being seen while running as a snow leopard? He was supposed to stay out of sight, or he'd have to run at night.

"Yeah, he was running in his fur coat. I thought—" Kolby shook his head and didn't finish what he had to say. "I'm a ranch hand at Hal Haverton's horse ranch. His property butts up to yours if you took over Wild Ridge Mansion. We can't see your place and you can't see ours from the ranch."

Which meant? Had her brother trespassed on the Haverton's property?

She scowled at her brother. He looked a little guilty, his ears tinged red. Then she turned her attention to Kolby and introduced herself and her brother to him. "Yes, we inherited the estate."

"That's good news. I'm Kolby Jones, by the way, and if you ever need any help with anything," he said, "just call on me." He pulled his business card out and handed it to her.

She looked at the card. It said he trained horses and gave horse trail rides, and it had his phone number and email address. She pulled out her business card and handed it to him.

He smiled. "A writer. That's so cool."

"Yes, and Eric's an artist."

"I left my business cards at home," Eric said.

He didn't have any because she couldn't get him to make any!

Mrs. Fitz suddenly returned, and Rosalie realized she'd been gone until now. She was carrying a sack of sandwiches and a tray with Eric and Rosalie's sandwiches also. "Could you use a refill on your drinks?" she asked Rosalie and Eric.

"I could," Eric said, waving his hand in front of his face as if he were burning up from all the heat that had erupted between Kolby and Rosalie. "It's getting hot in here."

Rosalie gave her brother a look to cool it. He ignored her as if he hadn't said anything wrong. Kolby just smiled at him, appearing amused at her brother's antics.

Ava hurried out to refill their drinks and Mrs. Fitz set Rosalie and Eric's sandwiches in front of them, then handed Kolby a large sack of sandwiches to go. Rosalie smelled all kinds of different sandwiches in the sack. "Here you are, Kolby."

Kolby turned his attention back to Rosalie, seeming to want to stay awhile now. But it looked like he had a lot of food for some hungry ranch hands most likely. "If you need help with anything, just call, text, or email me," he reiterated. "I've got to get these back to the ranch before the other guys think I ate them all."

She smiled. He was cute. He winked at her and headed for the door. Kolby was too charming for his own good.

She turned to face her brother. "You trespassed on the Halverton's property? You didn't tell me that anyone saw you on your run."

Eric shrugged. "He's a cougar, so no big deal at all." He bit into his sandwich. "Besides, like I said, you'll meet some guy like that who's falling all over himself over you and then where will I be?"

"Your mother said you were from Alaska. And she said your

father had snow leopard friends up there. We'll make inquiries. I'm sure we'll find more snow leopards too. But you know you might meet someone here that you really like who is sweet on you. Besides, I'm not abandoning you, so get used to the idea."

Eric scoffed, looking as though he didn't believe her, then began eating his sandwich some more. "Watch him be a member of the welcoming committee."

Rosalie could only hope! "You love horses, Eric. Maybe you can ride some of the horses sometime. You could even buy one and board it at their stables. It says on the card that they board horses there." She took a breath. "That's why you went in the direction of the ranch, isn't it? You wanted to see the horses." She should have known it had to do with something like that and not that he was trying to get himself into trouble. In his fantasy artwork, he often featured majestic horses and elves and the fae. "But you know if the ranchers had seen you, they might have worried you would try to kill one of their horses."

"Nah. They'd try to capture the wild exotic animal." Eric took another bite of his sandwich. At least he seemed to be enjoying the food here or she wouldn't have heard the last of it.

"And then where would we be?"

"You'd be in a haunted mansion all on your own," Eric said.

"It's not haunted."

Once they finished their sandwiches, Ava brought their desserts.

"If we did host the Halloween party, is there a theme?" Rosalie asked.

Eric's mouth parted.

"Nope. It's up to you," Ava said.

"Spell casters then."

"Wait, you can't be serious," Eric said.

"Yeah, we need to do this." Rosalie had decided. If the town was full of cougars, he needed to meet a bunch of them, and so did she. Maybe some of the local cougars had teens who could befriend him, and he wouldn't feel so isolated.

Maybe she could see more of Kolby Jones too.

But first things first. She and Eric needed to retrieve his clothes where he'd ditched them and hope the bear wasn't around any longer!

3

K olby was excited to meet the new cougar who was living so close to the Haverton's property. Hopefully, she wasn't seeing someone because he was totally interested in dating her. He couldn't figure out the relationship between her and the snow leopard though. Eric was definitely a teen with an attitude. The boy hadn't liked seeing Kolby speaking with her, but Kolby wasn't one to be discouraged when he wanted something.

As soon as he arrived at the ranch, the guys were eager to have lunch. They often splurged once a week eating takeout from Mrs. Fitz's shop or one of the other restaurants. He was so glad he was the one who had gone to get the meals this time. Otherwise, the other ranch hands would have met Rosalie and her brother first and might have made a better impression on her.

Hal's Australian shepherds, Zula and Koda, came over to greet Kolby and he petted them. "I wasn't gone that long, silly dogs."

Ted Weekum, their foreman, came over to say, "Hey, so I hear we have new neighbors."

Word sure spread fast among the local cougar population. "Yeah, I saw Eric running as a snow leopard on our property earlier today, but I hadn't wanted to say anything because I figured it was just a figment of my imagination." Kolby ran his hands through his hair, thinking he was in trouble now for not reporting it to anyone.

To Kolby's surprise, Ted laughed. "Yeah, like me seeing my Stella in her white cougar coat."

Oh, yeah, Kolby had forgotten about that. "That's true. That was unusual enough, but a snow leopard?"

"Mrs. Fitz said that his sister is a cougar though. I wonder how that came about."

"Step siblings, don't you think? The teen is a bit hostile. I was thinking if he doesn't have a father around to help him sort things out, we could get him out here to mentor him."

Ted smiled. "Like a big brother?"

"Yeah."

"Good luck with that," Ted said.

"No, wait. Not me. You."

Ted got a call from Hal and he looked at Kolby and raised his brows. "Yeah, Kolby met the filly already and from what I've heard from Mrs. Fitz, he's already staking a claim."

Kolby felt his face warm with chagrin. He shook his head. They might not be members of a wolf pack, but the cougars were like one big family in Yuma Town and in the surrounding area. It didn't take long for the word to get out that there were a couple of new cats in town. Or that one of them happened to be a snow leopard.

"Yeah. We can sure help with that. I'll send Kolby over there to handle it." Ted smiled at him.

Kolby frowned. Now what?

"All right. Talk to you later, Hal." Ted ended the call and slapped Kolby on the back. "You're in charge of helping Miss

Rosalie and her brother set up the Halloween party at their estate. You'll coordinate everything with everyone to make this happen."

"Why me?" That was one tall order for anyone to take on and Kolby really didn't know if he could handle all of it.

"You keep asking for more responsibility."

"Yeah, here, at the horse ranch."

"Well, this is mighty important."

Kolby sighed.

"While you're at it, let Rosalie and Eric know you're willing to mentor Eric."

"Oh, I'm sure that will go over well with the boy. Not."

"You know everyone, so coordinating with folks concerning the party won't be a problem at all. You work well with everyone, and you'll do a great job. Not only that, but you already oversee all the new ranch hands, and they really look up to you. It'll be the same with Eric. Just you see. See if Rosalie needs any help on the place. Make a list so we can take care of it."

"What about my work here?"

"When you don't have work to do at her place, getting things ready for the Halloween party, you can see what needs to be done here. But the party takes priority."

Kolby couldn't believe it. Since he'd begun working here and had a real purpose in life, just like his brother had when he worked here until Ricky became a deputy sheriff, he'd been happy. But being the event coordinator for a Halloween party and working with a she-cat he didn't truly know? He suspected he'd have trouble with her brother. Mentoring him? Being a big brother to him? He speculated that wasn't happening.

Sure, he'd helped set up the Halloween party for when it had been held at the ranch, but that meant decorating it. He hadn't been in charge of food or coordinating decorations or the games either. Except for horsey rides for little ones.

He figured he better call Rosalie and see if she was home. He could drop by and check out the place to see where they could set things up. Then he'd have a better idea what they'd need for the party too.

He pulled out her business card and called her. "Hey, it's me, Kolby Jones. My boss, Hal Haverton, just gave me the job of coordinating the Halloween party at your place. Would it be too inconvenient if I dropped by and looked it over to see what needs to be done?"

"Uh, yeah, sure. I have to warn you it's pretty dusty and cobwebby here, and we have tons of boxes everywhere that we haven't started unpacking."

"We have two months to whip it into shape and everyone will offer to help. I'm on my way over now."

"Okay, we'll see you soon."

ROSALIE HAD BOUGHT a boy and girl scarecrow and mini quilt from Mrs. Fitz's shop and set them on a window seat in the breakfast nook. Eric just shook his head as they unpacked their dishes and other kitchen items. They were trying to get the kitchen set up the way they liked it. Rosalie had taught him how to do laundry, cook, clean, and help do yardwork once their parents had died. He didn't care for cooking all that much since he'd become a teen, but she'd told him that women really liked a guy who could cook. He wasn't totally convinced.

"Don't tell me. That was Kolby, right?" Eric asked, drying the dishes she was washing.

"Yes. He's been put in charge of coordinating the Halloween event here. He's dropping by to see what needs to be done before the event."

"He can wash dishes."

"He's not coming here to do all our chores."

"If he really wants to be your boyfriend, he needs to do whatever he can to please you," Eric said, matter-of-factly, as if he had a wealth of experience in the dating field.

"Okay, look, if you met a girl and she came over to see you, would you expect her to wash dishes with you?" Rosalie asked, attempting to teach him a lesson of sorts. Though after she said it, she realized she shouldn't have because it sounded like she saw Kolby as her boyfriend. Which she didn't!

Ignoring her, Eric asked, "Did you ask him if there are any kids my age here?" He sounded hopeful and she realized he really did want to make some friends.

She sure hoped he could. "No. But you can ask him yourself and you can ask him about taking riding lessons too." Eric didn't say anything, and she figured he wanted *her* to query Kolby about everything. And she would. Eric could be shy around people he didn't know. Snarky, but shy.

As soon as they heard a Jeep pull up out in front of the mansion, Rosalie went outside to greet Kolby. At least that's who she figured had parked out front.

It *was* Kolby. He was all smiles and she felt really good about all this. She was getting so used to her brother's scowls that it was nice to see someone who was cheerful.

"This place is amazing. It has such possibilities," Kolby said, looking over the outside.

"That's what I thought. I know you have some places where people can stay the night in Yuma Town, but if I could ever get the mansion refurbished, we could offer some rooms too."

"Absolutely. We've had overflow spill into people's homes even. So that would be great."

She led Kolby inside the mansion, already feeling really good about his being here. The way he'd looked at the place made it seem like there was real hope for it too. Because Eric was so down about the mansion, she had begun to feel she was the only one who thought it had possibility.

"It looks big on the outside, but inside it's huge," Kolby said.

The marble tile floor of the foyer, the big windows on either side of the big door, the chandelier up above, were just stunning.

Rosalie agreed. "Yeah, it's really beautiful, well, once it's cleaned up a bit. It needs some updating."

"Chase Buchanan does amazing woodwork, refinishing, and the like. He and his mate, Shannon, own the Pinyon Pine Resort cabins at Lake Buchanan. He's also a deputy sheriff, so woodworking is really a hobby of his."

"For free?" Eric asked, coming out of the kitchen, carrying the damp dish towel.

"Of course not," Rosalie said, casting her brother an annoyed look to mind his manners.

"I'm sure you want to talk in private. I need to set up my bed for the night." Eric handed the dish towel to Kolby and ran up the stairs.

"Eric!" Rosalie scolded, so exasperated with her brother. If he kept acting like this, he'd never make any friends.

Eric ignored her as he pounded up the stairs.

She reached out to take the dish towel from Kolby, but he shook his head. "I can help while we talk and then we can look at where we can hold the event."

"All right. Well, here's the kitchen," she said, leading him into the huge kitchen. It was meant to feed a lot of people. "It needs an overhaul. We were just washing the dishes we unpacked so we could set up the kitchen a bit for meals. We bought groceries in Yuma Town and have stored them, but we really need to update all the appliances, install a dishwasher, etcetera. Then this would be great for having parties."

"Oh, yeah, this could end up being the party place."

Rosalie laughed. "Here I thought we were moving into the mansion to get away from people."

"Hopefully, you'll enjoy living and playing among the cougars here." Kolby set the dish towel on the countertop and brought out his phone and started making notes.

She began washing dishes again.

"Can I help you with this?" he asked.

"With cleaning the dishes?" She was surprised he'd offer.

"Sure, but with ordering the appliances? When Tracey mated Hal Haverton, she had the bunkhouse completely renovated. Ted Weekum, the foreman, my brother, Ricky, and I helped pick out what we needed in the kitchen to make it work great for a bunch of ranch hands."

Well, that was embarrassing that she assumed Kolby was offering to help with the dishes. But assistance with updating the kitchen appliances? That was much appreciated. "Yeah, sure."

He brought out a small tape measure and began taking measurements of all the appliances, the counterspace, and the sink location. She realized he was drawing a diagram of everything on his phone. She was impressed as she continued to wash utensils and dry them. Here she'd thought he was just a ranch hand, tending to horses and the like.

"Okay, you could use a double oven. I see you have a countertop microwave oven, but we could have one built in to keep your counters free of clutter."

"That sounds good."

Eric slipped into the kitchen to grab a soda from the fridge. "He's not washing the dishes?"

"He's helping us with plans to update the kitchen, which is much more important. Besides, it's your job to assist me with the dishes."

"Make sure the updated kitchen has a dishwasher," Eric said, and left again.

Kolby smiled.

Rosalie sighed. "I've been raising my stepbrother on my own since he was ten and I was twenty. He's been great until he turned thirteen. Then the teen attitude kicked in."

"He needs a mentor. A big brother."

She turned to face Kolby. "Can you teach him horseback riding?"

"Yeah, I sure can. I teach all ages from little tykes to grown adults, from those with no experience to lots of it."

"My brother loves horses, but he's never ridden one."

"We'll have to rectify that." Kolby started drying the utensils she was washing.

"Another thing, are there any teens in the area about his age? He's fifteen but turning sixteen in a week."

"Hell, yeah. Bobby Mayflower is thirteen, a little younger, but he's used to doing things with the older kids. He just had a birthday a week ago. His dad is a news reporter, and his mom is a dispatcher for the sheriff's office. April Hightower is the clinic receptionist, and she has a daughter, Cathy, and a son, Sonny, who are fifteen and a half. Nurse Elsie Miller has a daughter, Sissy, who is fifteen. Becky, who is the emergency operator at the clinic, and her husband, Steele Sorenson have a son and daughter, Andy and Avery who are sixteen and a half."

"Oh, wonderful. He's got to meet them."

"Are you homeschooling Eric?" Kolby asked.

"Yeah. He couldn't sit still in school. He'd get too antsy and wanted to run as a cat. If someone angered him, he'd want to show his claws...and his teeth. So his mom was homeschooling him until she died and then I took over."

"The group of teens meet with different community

members to learn skills as part of their homeschool curriculum. He would be welcome to join them."

"Oh, wonderful." She hoped she could convince Eric to join them. "If anyone wants me to teach creative writing, I can do that."

"I'm sure everyone would love that."

If Eric would go to the various activities, he could meet some of the kids, but she was afraid he'd decline. "He loves home-schooling online."

"That's fine. But he could supplement his schooling with the activities the other kids do. Like for instance, horseback riding lessons, horse care, ranching. But also, so many cougars have interesting occupations, and they teach the kids about them. Like banking, culinary crafts, swimming, woodworking, just some new skills all the kids enjoy." Kolby started working on washing the pots and pans.

She smiled at him. Was he for real? Or did he just add the horseback riding to the curriculum to try and win her brother over? Once Kolby helped her finish with the kitchen wares and putting away the rest of the grocery items that hadn't needed refrigeration, she led him into one of the huge dining rooms that had several tables and chairs for seating for nearly two-hundred people.

"This is the Rose Room."

"Wow, this will be great," Kolby said.

"Yeah, the tables and chairs are beautiful. Dusty, but every-thing is." She took him into the smaller dining room. "The Orchid Room seats nearly a hundred people."

Smiling, he just shook his head. "This is incredible."

"We also have six meeting rooms, but we're using one for an art studio and one for my office space to write my books. We also have twelve guest rooms. Well, two of them serve as our bedrooms."

The ballroom was next. "It's 2200 square feet and can hold up to 240 people," she said.

His mouth gaped. "This is fantastic. It's perfect for the dance floor. We can set up a live band right over there, grazing tables to snack on foods, or people can go to the dining room of your choosing and can sit down with their food and eat."

"That sounds good." She was thinking that the party could really be fun and bring some life into the place. "There are three bathrooms on the first floor and bathrooms in each of the bedrooms on the second floor, so we're set there."

"Okay, good." He looked around at the cobwebs hanging from the crystal chandelier.

"It's halfway decorated for Halloween," she said, facetiously.

Kolby smiled. "We can leave them up, if you want, but after the party? We'll remove them for you."

"Oh, wonderful." She wasn't sure she wanted them up for that long though.

"Can I talk to Eric about the horseback riding class we give?" Kolby asked.

"Yeah, sure. He's up in the tower room on the fourth floor. He's been a loner of a necessity, so it might take some work to bring him out of his shell."

"I totally understand that." Kolby headed up the creaking stairs to the tower room and Rosalie watched him for a moment, praying that Eric would give this opportunity to meet the others a chance.

4

———————

Kolby sure hoped talking to Eric would work. He and his brother had lost their own parents when they were younger and he had helped to raise his younger brother, Ricky. So he knew something of what both Eric and Rosalie were going through. Though he and his brother had been human, not shifters at the time.

He knocked on the door frame to Eric's room where Eric was lying on his bed, wearing headphones, listening to music. Eric pulled off his headphones and looked over at Kolby.

"Hey, sorry to interrupt, but Rosalie said you would like to take horseback riding lessons and meet the other teens who are your age. It's part of a homeschooling program. We have a lot of different activities for kids of all ages."

Eric sat up in bed, looking warily interested.

"You can join us at ten tomorrow morning, if you'd like to participate. No cost. We have a wealthy benefactor who promotes learning among our kids."

"Cougars."

Kolby sighed. "Yeah, but they're shifters like you and that makes them more like you than humans are. Not only that, but we've had caracal shifters in the area before. So, though you're new to us, we've had other kinds of unusual shifters. Bears even. Ted's mate is a rare white cougar. A wolf came through here also. So we're all unusual in our own way."

"Oh, wow, I didn't know about the other shifters. Wait. A bear, uhm, was sniffing at my clothes and I thought it was all bear. I need to get my clothes that are a couple of acres away from the mansion. We were going to wait until the coast was clear."

"It can be one of the shifters we've met. They're good guys. Do you want me to go with you to help you get your clothes?"

"Hell, yeah." Eric hurried off the bed, looking relieved. "They're my favorite jeans and hiking boots. Oh, and yeah, going to the horseback riding lessons sounds great."

Kolby thought he was getting through to the teen a little bit. The problem was that Kolby would have to set this whole horseback riding class up in a hurry. He knew Ted and Hal would have a good laugh over it.

"If Rosalie can drive me there for it, I'll come."

"I can drive you there!" Rosalie called from the bottom of the stairs.

Kolby smiled. Cat hearing. "If you ever need a ride to any of the activities, just let me know and we'll take care of it."

"Uh, yeah, sure, thanks."

So it appeared that Eric was interested in something. He told him about all the teens that lived in the area and Eric smiled.

"They're great kids. They'll be excited to meet you. But I'll apologize first in the event they want to see you in your snow leopard coat. None of us have seen a snow leopard shifter before," Kolby said.

Eric smiled and Kolby thought he might be feeling better about the notion that he was going to be someone special among the cougar teens.

"Okay, well, I've got to get out of here and begin work on helping you all with the updates on the estate and start coordinating with others to set up the party. So let's get your clothes, all right?" Kolby asked.

"Let me know what I can do to help." Eric headed downstairs with him.

Kolby was surprised to hear the young man offer.

"You can do some artwork," Rosalie said from the bottom of the stairs.

"I'll make ghosts out of sheets. But, yeah, I paint fantasy art," Eric said to Kolby. "Do you want to see some of my paintings?"

"Yeah, sure." Kolby hoped he still had time to rearrange everyone's schedules for the impromptu, horseback riding training tomorrow, but he knew how important this was to Eric for him to see his accomplishments. Kolby hadn't expected much of anything but some juvenile artwork when he walked into Eric's art studio, but man, the kid had talent. "These are beautiful. Can we commission you for one of your horse paintings?" Eric painted the most beautiful horse scenes, fantasy, sure, extraordinarily, fantastical art.

Eric's whole expression brightened. "Oh, yeah, sure. Just tell me what colors you want and the kind of scene, and I can do it."

"Okay, let me think on it. I'll get back with you." Kolby said to Rosalie, "Do you have a dollar budget for your appliances?"

"We've got the money, so that's truly no object."

"All right. Well, I'll talk to some folks, and I'll check in with you to see what you would like to get."

"But you're all set with Eric going horseback riding and meeting the other teens?" Rosalie asked.

Absolutely not, but as soon as he got in his Jeep, Kolby was getting this done, even if he had to bribe a whole bunch of people. "Yeah, sure."

"I'll go with the two of you to get Eric's clothes. I want to be able to learn the bear's scent, and know whether it's a bear or a shifter," Rosalie said.

"Sure," Kolby said.

The three of them left the house and took off on a hike to the location of Eric's clothes. When they reached them, Kolby said, "It's Blue Bearsden. His first name is really Joh, but he goes by Blue. He probably was intrigued that he smelled the snow leopard's scent on your clothes, Eric. But if you see him again, at least you'll know who he is—in bear form or by scent."

"Okay, that's good to know," Rosalie said.

"Yeah." Eric bundled his clothes together and they headed back to the mansion.

Once they reached the mansion, Kolby got into his Jeep, and Eric lovingly ran his hand over the hood before Kolby said goodbye. "I'll talk to you soon."

Then he drove off, waving goodbye. Kolby believed he'd actually reached Eric a little. He hoped he didn't screw up the small success he'd made so far. He couldn't help but be thrilled that Rosalie was so relieved that he was getting her brother interested in something.

As soon as Kolby drove down the road, he called Ted. "Hey, Kolby here. We need to set up a horse-riding lesson for Eric with the other teens his age at a homeschooling activity for ten tomorrow morning."

Ted laughed. "You'd better get cracking on it. It sounds like you're getting a good start on mentoring Eric."

Ah, hell, Kolby should have known Ted would leave the job to him. Kolby quickly called the parents of the teens in question and put them on a conference call. "Hey, this is Kolby. I know it's really short notice, but can all your teens come to the Haverton ranch to do horseback riding lessons at ten? I want them to meet the new teen in town, Eric Squire, who has moved into Wild Ridge Mansion. He's fifteen, going on sixteen, and he wants riding lessons, but he also wants to meet others his age."

"The boy who's a snow leopard?" April Hightower asked. "Oh, absolutely. Cathy and Sonny are excited to meet him."

"My Avery and Andy are also," Becky Sorenson said.

"Bobby also," Deacon Mayflower said, his wife, Amy agreeing.

Sissy's mother, Elsie Miller, also confirmed that Sissy would love to go horseback riding any time.

"Okay, well, he's never been horseback riding, so I want everyone to know that ahead of time. He does beautiful fantasy artwork, so that might be something everyone can talk to him about."

"Don't worry," Becky said. "The kids will come up with topics on their own. Hopefully it won't be all about asking if the mansion is haunted, but you know some of that will come up."

"Yeah, I wouldn't be surprised. Also, his older sister, Rosalie, writes a published spell caster series and she said she would be interested in teaching the kids some creative writing," Kolby said.

"Oh, that would be wonderful. Cathy is always writing short stories," April said.

"That would be a great addition to their curriculum," Becky said.

And that was it. Kolby thought he wasn't too bad at this after all. It helped to have a group of cougars who could provide a unified force whenever they needed them to. Then they ended the call and he arrived at the ranch and parked his Jeep. Ted waved at him and came over to speak with him. "We've got the horses and we're free at ten for the riding lessons you're going to give."

"Thanks, Ted. I arranged it with the parents. The kids are all eager to meet Eric."

"Good show. I knew you could do it."

Kolby sure hadn't been certain.

"So how did the inspection of the estate go?" Ted asked.

"It went great. The place will be perfect for the party. But she needs to have all her appliances changed out. I'll be helping her with that."

Ted smiled. "Fantastic. If you need any advice, just ask. And you know how Tracey is. She's good at figuring out stuff like that. So ask her for some ideas too."

"Okay, I will." Kolby would take all the input he could get. He called Rosalie back. "Hey, it's me, Kolby. Everyone's eager to meet Eric tomorrow and they're also up for you to work with their teens on creative writing."

"Oh, wow, okay. I've taught some writing classes at libraries for kids before, so that will be fun."

Kolby was glad he had been able to set things up so that Rosalie and her brother would feel like they were more part of the cougar community. "Okay, I've got to check out some resources on your kitchen appliances and get back with you." Here he was thinking of dating her, and instead he was too busy to even ask her out. But maybe this worked even better. "Oh, what about a new washer and dryer also?"

"Yeah, we need the larger ones, industrial strength, to handle all the bedding in the mansion. Oh, I need to go. Someone's at the door, Kolby," Rosalie said.

"Okay, I'll talk to you later." Things were looking up with Rosalie, Kolby thought. He couldn't be more thrilled about it.

∼

ROSALIE WAS SO glad she and Eric had gone to Mrs. Fitz's shop for lunch and met Kolby and that he was willing to help them out with so many chores. She had been setting up her office when Kolby called, and then she heard the doorbell ring. She hurried off to see who it was and answered the door.

"Hi, I'm Shannon Buchanan, and my husband and I own the resort on Lake Buchanan." She was striking with her golden eyes and dark hair, and she was carrying a beautiful basket filled with a bottle of cabernet, a variety of cheeses, and several kinds of crackers.

"Oh, yes, come inside," Rosalie said. "I understand your husband does woodworking."

"Exactly. Oh, this is a beautiful place. Chase would love to refinish things for you, if you'd like him to help you with it. He teaches kids wood crafting when he has time, and he could even bring a group out to help with it."

"That would be great." As long as the kids didn't destroy the beautiful wood.

"Oh, this is for you to welcome you to the neighborhood."

"Thanks so much. It looks wonderful. Would you like a soda?" Rosalie took the basket of goodies from her.

"Yeah, sure."

Rosalie took her in to see the kitchen and set the basket on the counter.

"Oh, my, this would be perfect for an 80's themed party," Shannon said.

"Right." Rosalie offered her a choice of drinks and Shannon took one. "I really need to update it."

"We can help with that," Shannon said.

Rosalie felt overwhelmed by the generosity of the Yuma Town residents. She'd never expected this. "Kolby offered too."

"Good. We'll coordinate with you and him on that. Believe me, if you want us to butt out at any time, just say so. You won't hurt our feelings. We just want to help you out, but we don't want you to feel we're being too intrusive."

"No, no, thinking of renovating this place is really overwhelming and I've never done anything like this, so I really appreciate everyone's help."

"Okay, great. But don't ever feel like we're taking over. We just want to assist. So what theme do you want to use for the Halloween party?" Shannon asked as Rosalie showed her the ballroom. "Oh, this is beautiful."

"It really is. It will make a great place for a party."

"Several." Shannon glanced up at the spiderweb-covered chandelier. "We would pay to have big celebrations here."

"Well—"

"We would insist on paying."

"All right." Rosalie smiled. What could be better than having venues here that were attended by all shifters? How much fun would that be? "On the theme, how about spell casters, wizards, warlocks, and witches?"

"That sounds like fun."

Eric came out of his art studio and said, "I finished getting my art room set up and started to paint again." Then he saw Shannon. "Oh, sorry, I didn't know you had company."

"Hi, I'm Shannon Buchanan. We all try to share our expertise in anything we do. If you would like, you could teach others about painting."

Eric beamed. "Would you like to see my artwork?"

"You bet." Shannon went with him, and Rosalie felt wonderful.

Everyone was really bringing her brother out of his shell. This was the best thing she could ever have done for him. She hadn't been sure at first when they moved in, and she saw how much work they had to do and how unhappy Eric had been about it.

She followed them into the art studio, wondering what he'd done with the room. He'd already hung several of his paintings on the walls featuring centaurs, winged horses, unicorns, elves, fae, beautifully illustrated scenes that made her feel she could fall into their worlds and live there.

He had his easel set up and all his paints were organized. She was always proud of how much he liked to keep things nice and neat, and it was perfect for showing off to anyone who visited.

Shannon just gaped at the paintings. "Oh, you've got to teach us how you paint. Not just the kids, but the adults who would love to learn how to paint, even if they can't create beautiful artwork like you. These are just stunning—the colors, the details, the realism."

"Thanks," Eric said.

Rosalie swore he hadn't smiled this much since he had turned thirteen. She was thrilled to see him happy for a change. She hoped he would like the other teens, and no one would make him feel subconscious because he was a snow leopard and not a cougar like them.

"I don't know how to teach it, but I guess I can learn," Eric said.

"You can do it, Eric. And it would be fun. Heck, I'd love to learn how to paint, even though I know I'd never be as good as you at it," Rosalie said.

"No way, sis. You buy covers from me when you write your strictly fantasy stories. I don't want to lose that book cover market."

Rosalie laughed. He could be cute when he wanted to be.

"Well, I'm really excited about this. And having the party here. I need to get back to my place, but I just wanted to welcome you here and to the Yuma Town family," Shannon said, finishing her soda.

Rosalie thanked her for coming by and bringing the house-warming gift, then saw her to the door. "You made my brother's day, by the way," she said quietly to her.

"His artwork is beautiful. He'll inspire others with it."

"He'll be thrilled about it."

Then they said goodbye and Rosalie went back to work on cleaning up the room where she would create her stories. The internet was working great. She had worried about that.

She was back to work on the room when the doorbell rang again. She hurried off to see who it was this time. An older woman. When Rosalie opened the door to her, the woman smiled warmly.

"Hi, I'm Mae Sorenson, some call me the cat lady. My momma cat, Spooks, had kittens and they're two months' old now. Since you're living out here in a big old estate, I wondered if you could give one a home?" She pulled out her phone and showed her a picture of the all black kittens.

"Aww, they're adorable."

"I brought them with me. They're ready for a home."

Rosalie smiled. There was no way she could turn down a cat. She hadn't had one for years and with this big old place, it would be perfect.

Then her brother came out to see who the new visitor was, and Mae smiled at him. "You're the new snow leopard in town. Everyone is so excited about both of you taking over the old place."

"She's offering us a cat."

Mae said, "I'll bring them right in."

Smiling, Eric raised a brow at Rosalie. "I'm all for it," she said. "What about you?"

"We haven't had one in years. Yeah, I'm game."

Mae brought a basket of black kittens inside. Eric and Rosalie were smiling and talking to the kittens.

"We've got to have two of them so they can continue to socialize with each other," Rosalie said, knowing her brother wanted more than just one.

Eric laughed. "Yeah. Can we have two of them?" he asked Mae.

"You sure can. They'll have a ball exploring this big old place."

They picked out the two most playful of the litter and named the female Leia and Vader for the male.

"I'll be right back," Mae said. "I have a couple of starter packages that go with the kittens as your welcome gifts."

"I'll help you," Eric offered, while Rosalie watched the kittens playing in a jumble of legs.

When they returned to the house, they were carrying two cat litter boxes, kitty litter, food, squeaky, fuzzy play toys, and one climbing perch.

"Oh, wow, thanks so much," Rosalie said. She'd never expected all this.

"It's from me, but also from my son, Mick Sorenson, who is in charge of the department of Fish and Wildlife Services that Tracey and Hal Haverton work for, and my niece, Becky, and her teens, Avery and Andy."

"Thanks so much," Eric said, sitting on the floor, playing with all the kittens now.

"Can I fix you something to drink?" Rosalie belatedly asked.

"Thank you, but I need to get home to the rest of my babies. Thanks so much for giving two of them a home."

Eric helped Mae out with the basket of four kittens, while Rosalie held onto Leia and Vader, and they said their goodbyes.

"I love this place already," Eric said, returning to the mansion with Rosalie. "So where do we set up the kitty cat room? Can they be in my room at night?"

She smiled. "They sure can."

∿

ROSALIE AND ERIC had pizzas that night, and then they cleaned up and she sat on a chair in his bedroom in the tower for a while, playing with the kittens. Now she wished his room was closer to hers. The mansion was spooky at night. Though thankfully, their cat eyes could see well at night. "We can move your mattress to the bed in the room next to mine if you'd like."

"Are you scared?"

She smiled. "I might sleep as a cougar tonight."

He laughed. "I might sleep as a snow leopard. I think it's going to really work out well here for us. We'll see what happens tomorrow though."

"You'll be fine." At least she sure hoped so.

"Okay, I'm going to bed, but if you get lonely, let me know and I can curl up at the foot of your bed in my fur coat," Eric said.

"Ditto for me. If you find me sleeping on the foot of your bed, think nothing of it."

He chuckled. "Uhm, do you think there are any ghosts here?"

"No." She'd purposefully not brought up the notion of ghosts when they moved in. She didn't want him to worry about them. She really didn't think there were any here.

Then she finally retired to her bed while he went to sleep in his. Or at least she hoped he'd sleep just fine. She'd heard strange noises all day in the mansion, but it was a big place and even if it had just been a normal home, hearing strange noises wouldn't be unusual.

She'd done research about the old place and found the original owners had died there, both due to natural causes, two years apart, the husband dying after his wife had passed on.

She was surprised there hadn't been a lot of vandalism, but she wondered if that was due to the vigilance of the sheriff's department and the local community being all cougars.

She climbed under her sheets. She was glad she had her own bedding. She wouldn't have been able to breathe if she'd had to sleep on the original dusty bedding. Closing her eyes, she sighed. This had been one interesting and exciting day.

She heard the wind blowing against the window, knew it was cold out, but inside the mansion she was nice and warm. Tomorrow morning when it was still dark out, she wanted to run as a cougar with her brother. She had meant to tonight, but they had worked so hard on the house, that by the time it was dark, she was worn out. Eric, to her surprise, was too. So tomorrow, they would first thing, before Mrs. Fitz brought their breakfast and Eric took off for his riding lessons.

She was thinking about running with Kolby too. And other cougars also. But especially with Kolby. She was thinking Eric might want to run with his new friends also.

She was about to drift off to sleep when she heard Eric padding into her room on his big cat paws. She should have helped him move his mattress to the room next to hers. He might be nearly sixteen, but he was still a kid, and he appeared nervous about the new place.

She smiled at him and patted the bed. He leaped onto the bed and then she could sleep with him being near like that, just like he could.

Yet in the middle of the night something woke them both. Eric lifted his head then leapt off the bed. "I'll be right there with you," she said.

Eric left the room, and she pulled off her pajamas, felt the heat warming her muscles, her muscles stretching, and then she suddenly shifted and leaped from the bed. She ran into the hall where her brother was listening for whatever sound they'd heard that had woken them. She was glad he'd been with her.

The two of them moved quietly down the hall and she thought the sound had come from downstairs. She headed down the stairs, her paws silent, the stairs not creaking like when they walked down it as humans.

Eric was right behind her, his nose touching the tip of her tail from time to time when she flicked it past his face. He was sticking close to her, and she was glad he was.

They finally made it down to the bottom of the stairs and began searching each of the rooms downstairs—the kitchen, dining rooms, living area, ballroom, her office, his art studio, the library, the den, the foyer and the meeting rooms.

They didn't find anything or anyone. No scents other than Shannon's, Kolby's, and theirs. They continued to search until they came to the door to the basement.

Both of them paused. The door was shut to the basement. Old, dust-covered, metal file cabinets filled with former guest records before computers were down there. Some conference tables and chairs were stored in there, a woodworking workshop too. There were also a washing machine and dryer, a bathroom, and a bed on a metal frame in the basement.

She didn't remember what else was down there, but nothing she had thought was that important. She wondered if a racoon or something had found a way into the basement.

Her brother was standing next to her at the door, waiting for her to decide what to do.

5

Something crashed in the basement and both Rosalie and Eric jumped a little at the closed door. Eric growled. She shifted and saw that she couldn't lock the door. "Come on. I'm calling the sheriff's department. The basement door doesn't have a lock." She hadn't realized until that moment that she couldn't secure it.

Probably nothing but a wild animal had gotten in, but what if it wasn't? What if some man was living down there and he was an ax murderer or something? She wasn't about to go into the basement to check it out now.

She shifted and dashed for the stairs to get to her bedroom where her phone was.

But then she heard something running up the stairs in the basement, and her brother was still near the basement door as if he was frozen in time, listening, watching for it.

She raced back down the stairs, nipped at him, and then she ran to the front door with him right behind her. But the front cougar door was locked.

She shifted, fumbled with the lock, cursing under her breath, and then pulled open the latch to the cougar door. Shifting, she followed her brother out and he ran straight for the Haverton's ranch with her in hot pursuit. They would have to return for the kittens too.

KOLBY HEARD the sound of a cougar crying out and didn't recognize the voice. He was out of bed and in his cougar coat in a flash, racing for the door to come to the cat's aid, if it was a shifter. It was coming from the direction of the Wild Ridge Mansion.

Lights came on in the Havertons' ranch house as Kolby heard another cat's sound of distress, but not a cougar's call. Hell, it had to be Eric and Rosalie, and something had spooked them.

He called out in his cougar cry, telling them he was on his way to save them. They wouldn't recognize his voice either though.

It didn't take long for him to see Hal in his all-terrain vehicle and Ted riding shotgun, tearing across the property. Three of the ranch hands were in their cougar forms trying to catch up to them.

Kolby finally saw the cougar and snow leopard and he knew for sure they were Rosalie and Eric. He was glad they had come to them for help. He called out to her again and she cried out, sounding thankful for all the troops coming to assist them.

When Hal reached them, Eric shifted and shouted, "Something's in our basement and it was coming up the stairs. We didn't have any way to lock it, so we ran to you for help."

"We're heading that way," Hal said, and he and Ted had to drive to the main road then to reach the mansion.

Before Kolby reached Rosalie and her brother, she whipped around and tore off toward the fence. *Okay, so she wanted to see who had been in the house.* Her brother followed suit, and Kolby sprinted to catch up to them. He finally reached Rosalie and nuzzled her neck, hoping she wouldn't be annoyed with him, and he would get a nip for it, but she licked him back, appearing grateful for the rescue.

They saw the headlights of the ATV at the house. Hal and Ted were out of the vehicle but not making a move to go inside. Then Kolby heard the telltale sound of the sheriff's vehicles on the way. Deputy Chase Buchanan's, Kolby's brother, Ricky's, Stryker Hill's—or it might be his wife, Nina, or both, Sheriff Dan Steinacker, and well, Hal was already there as a part-time deputy.

Kolby was glad they all had come to take care of the threat and that his boss and the foreman hadn't tried to deal with this on their own.

Kolby was dying to go inside in the worst way to learn what was going on and yeah, he supposed he wanted to show what a hero he could be. Instead, he stayed with the ranch hands and Rosalie and her brother to watch out for them while the other deputy sheriffs and the sheriff arrived. Dan had Stryker, Ricky, and Ted go around the back. The sheriff wanted Nina to stay with Rosalie and her brother since she was armed with a 9mm in case anything got by the others.

Normally, Nina might have been peeved that she couldn't be just one of the guys, but everyone knew she and her mate, Stryker, were trying to get pregnant, and no one wanted her to get injured on the job. Stryker kept saying it could be any day now. Nina looked ready to sock him every time he said it. Everyone just chuckled about it.

Dan used lockpicks to unlock the front door, then he, Hal, and Chase went in the front way. "Sheriff's department!" Dan called out.

Kolby was as tense as the others were who were staying put,

though he sure still wished he could be inside checking things out.

No one responded. They could hear the men moving around in the mansion, a big place, so it would take a while to search all the rooms, under the beds, in the closets, and every place else.

Kolby wanted to take Rosalie and her brother back to the ranch house to chill out until the mansion was declared clear, but he knew she wouldn't want to leave until they learned what was in the house.

After what seemed like forever, Dan and Chase came out of the mansion. Dan shook his head. "We didn't find anything."

Eric shifted. "No way. It was coming up the stairs. But we have to save the kittens too." Then he shifted back into his snow leopard coat. It was too cold out here to stay in human form for long when he wasn't wearing anything.

Kolby was proud of Eric for doing all the talking though, and not making his sister shift to tell them what was going on. He suspected she might be a little shy if she wasn't used to shifting in front of other cougars. Most had grown up doing so, and it wasn't any big deal to them. But she and her brother had been on their own for a long time, so that could make a difference. Plus, Kolby swore Eric was trying to make a good impression on him.

Hal, Stryker, and Ted were still in the house. Kolby wondered what they were doing.

"We need to replace the doorknob on the basement door so it'll lock. We didn't smell or see anything," Dan said. "Hal said you can stay with them for the night. The kittens too. We can escort you inside and you can shift, dress, and pack a bag, and then you can either follow us home in your vehicle or we'll drive you there. Chase and Stryker are staying here for the rest of the night in case anything else happens."

Rosalie nodded and headed into the mansion, her brother following.

Dan smiled at Kolby. "I hear you have a couple of new jobs. Mentoring Eric and setting up the Halloween party. Well, and helping her with updating her place. Why don't you go in and have a look around and see if you notice anything out of the ordinary since you were here earlier."

Kolby growled his assent and headed into the house. He was so glad Dan gave him the opportunity to check things out for them, not that he'd find anything if they hadn't. But he hadn't smelled kittens in the mansion before, so he wondered about that.

He loped into the foyer, and then to the basement. The door was wide open, and the light was on downstairs. He made his way cautiously down the stairs, expecting something to jump out of the shadows at him at any moment.

He smelled around the place but didn't notice any unusual scents like that of a racoon or anything else down here. He didn't know what to think. He believed that Rosalie and Eric had heard something. But something climbing up the stairs? Ghosts came to mind. Stryker and his twin brother, Leyton, and Chase could actually see ghosts, if Chase was doing a séance. Kolby wondered if they'd felt any presences. His fur was standing up on end as he made his way to the bottom of the stairs and then he began searching every corner of the room and found a door that led outside. He shifted and checked the door, but when he turned the knob, he found it was locked. He heard someone on the stairs and turned to see who it was and saw Rosalie staring at him. He smiled and shifted into his cougar.

She smiled a little and descended the stairs, looking around like he had, probably not believing that no one had found a thing unless she saw it for herself. "We knew what we heard," she finally said after checking out every nook and cranny.

He growled at her in agreement.

When she didn't find anything, she motioned to the stairs. He let her go up first though. Once she climbed the stairs part way, he followed her up. They left the basement and saw her brother waiting with their bags and Stryker.

"Are you ready to go to the ranch house?" Stryker asked.

"Is someone really staying here the night?" she asked.

"Yeah. We'll have a couple of people here overnight, just in case someone or something comes in the middle of the night."

"Okay, good. Because something or someone *was* coming up those stairs in the basement," Rosalie said.

"Unless it was a ghost," her brother said, holding onto a kitty litter box.

"There are no ghosts here," she said, frowning at her brother. She grabbed up a cat carrier and Kolby saw two black kittens peering back at him through one of the grated windows.

Kolby wasn't so sure there weren't any ghosts here. She and her brother got into Dan's sheriff's car. Kolby and the other ranch hands in their fur coats raced back to the bunkhouse. Kolby wanted Rosalie to stay at the ranch house with him! But he figured she'd stay with her brother with Tracey and Hal instead.

When he and the other ranch hands reached the bunkhouse, they went single file in through the cougar door. Then he went to his room, shifted, and ran his hands through his hair. The other ranch hands went to bed, knowing their day started before dawn. But Kolby couldn't sleep.

Then someone knocked on the bunkhouse door and he threw on some boxer briefs and hurried down the hall to answer it, figuring it was Hal. When he opened the door, he saw Rosalie standing in the door frame, surprising him. He was certain she would spend the night with the Havertons. He glanced around her, but she was alone. He guessed she wanted to talk then instead.

"Do you want to come in?" He was confused.

"Yeah." She walked into the living room, and he shut the door.

"You're staying at the Havertons' right?" he asked.

"Yes. I have to know the truth though. Is the mansion haunted?"

Kolby led her to the sofas and they both took a seat. "I...don't have any paranormal abilities, unless you call shifting into a cougar paranormal."

She dismissed the comment with a wave of her hand. "That's natural for us. This is paranormal." She created a glowing ball in her hands, the yellow light reflecting off her face.

Openmouthed, he just stared at it. "What...how...how did you do that? Is it a trick?"

"No. I've been able to conjure up light since I was little. My biological mom and dad had to hide my ability from others until I learned to control it. Just like hiding that we could turn into cougars."

"Wow, uh, so what can you do with it?"

"It's a light, Kolby, that's all."

But he thought she might be hiding more about it, afraid to show him what she really could do. Create a light? Make a fireball? His imagination was going wild here.

"I want to know if the mansion house is haunted."

Kolby cleared his throat. "Okay, if Chase, you know, the deputy sheriff, has a séance, he can sometimes summon spirits. Stryker, the other deputy, and his brother whom you haven't met, Leyton, also can see ghosts."

"Oh, wow. Then I'm talking to the wrong guy."

That hurt.

"So that's why Chase and Stryker were the two who were selected to stay overnight then."

"Yeah, I suspect that's why Dan chose them to stay overnight. Hey, I believe you that you heard something in the basement." But Kolby was on the fence about ghosts. Or at least in this case. He suspected someone had been in the house. Or something. Rats even.

"If it wasn't a ghost, then what?"

"The door to the basement was locked to the outside," Kolby said.

She let out her breath.

"But what if someone had a key to it? Or had even used a lockpick to gain entry that way?" he asked.

"We didn't smell any sign of anyone in the basement."

Kolby sighed. "Right. But what if someone wore hunter's concealment scent?"

Her jaw dropped. Kolby wanted to run his hand through her red hair, to feel its silkiness, to smell the strands that he caught a whiff of when she was standing in the doorway, of peaches and honey.

"Why? Who would it be?"

"A drifter? Someone with a set of lockpicks, sleeping in the basement on cold nights?" He really didn't know, but yeah, he was concerned.

"Why not in one of the beds? Why wear hunter's concealment scent?" Rosalie asked.

"Yeah, that doesn't make any sense. Unless he believed that some of the sheriff's people would check out the place from time to time and smell that he—or frankly, she—had been there."

Rosalie glanced at his boxer shorts.

"Sorry, I had to answer the door quickly. I had no idea who it was."

"You probably have to get up really early."

"I do, but this is important."

"Thanks for coming to my rescue."

He smiled. "You're welcome."

She sighed. "I need to get back to the Havertons' house."

"Or you could stay here. With me tonight." Kolby raised his brows.

She laughed.

"No, huh? I'll walk you back to the ranch house."

"No need. It's not that far from here."

"I've been taught better than that," Kolby said.

"You're going like that?"

"Will you wait?" Kolby sounded a little desperate to walk her to the Halvertons' place. But that was the only decent thing to do.

"Yeah, sure." She smiled at him.

He leapt off the sofa and raced to his bedroom. As fast as he could, he dressed in pants, boots, and a sweater, then hurried back to join her.

"Wow, that was quick."

He smiled. "Come on. Let's go." He opened the door to the bunkhouse and let her out in the chilly air. Then he walked her to the ranch house. "I can stay at the mansion with you both, if you'd like and try to figure this out just in case it happens again."

"Tomorrow night."

"Yeah. We have others at the house tonight to watch things."

"Uhm, okay."

"Hot damn," Kolby said.

She chuckled. "I know the others won't want to stay at the mansion with us beyond tonight."

"I'll stay as long as it takes to reveal the mystery."

"Okay, thanks. We appreciate it."

He would do anything to ingratiate himself with Rosalie and her brother.

When they reached the Havertons' porch, the light still on, she pulled Kolby into her arms and smiled. "I hope you don't have a girlfriend. If so, she's out of luck."

Kolby laughed and wrapped his arms around her and kissed her. "I don't." Her lips parted for his and she kissed him back, tongues teasing and tasting, and then they deepened their kiss, tongues sliding leisurely over each other's. Oh, man, he wished she'd agreed to stay with him tonight.

She pulled away slightly. "Hmm. Thanks for everything, Kolby. Night."

"Night, Rosalie. I'll stay at your place for as long as you need me to. And we've got to come up with a date night."

She smiled. "You have a movie theater. Take me to the movies."

"You've got it."

Then they said good night again and she headed inside the house and locked the door.

Oh, man, seeing the snow leopard hadn't been a figment of his imagination. Things were getting so much more real. He had himself a girlfriend! And was mentoring her younger brother. He'd never expected such a strange twist of fate. Now this business with the strange occurrence at the mansion? He had to solve the mystery.

6

Ohmigod, Kolby was such a hottie! Rosalie closed and locked the door and saw her brother standing at the window where he'd been watching her and Kolby.

"He's okay, I guess," Eric said.

She let out her breath. "You were supposed to be in bed, like I was going to be."

"I just wanted to see what you had to say to Kolby. I'm not sure you were doing a lot of talking though."

She smiled. "I asked him if he thought the place was haunted. But he offered to stay with us to help us solve the mystery."

"He believed us." Eric sounded surprised.

"Yeah. He said that the person might have been wearing hunter concealment spray."

"What?" Eric said.

"Yeah."

"Why? Unless...unless he is a shifter."

"Exactly. Come on. Let's go to bed."

"So Kolby is staying in your room the night?" Eric asked.

"We have ten other bedrooms."

"That are dusty and dirty." Eric took a huge breath and then let it out. "He could stay with you, but then what if I got scared?"

She smiled and hugged her brother. "You can just jump on my bed in your snow leopard coat like you did tonight."

He chuckled and hugged her back. "I'm sure he would love that." He frowned. "Did you tell him about your special abilities? That might be the end of your new relationship, you know."

She sighed. "Yeah. He thought it was cool."

Her brother raised a brow.

"I didn't tell him *everything* I could do with my abilities."

"Then *what*?"

"That I can produce a ball of light."

Eric shook his head. "That's only the tip of the iceberg."

She knew that! Which is why she hadn't mentioned all the rest. She figured she'd ease Kolby into everything else as time went on.

Then she and her brother went to their separate rooms, he had the kittens in his room, and she was glad that tonight they would feel safe and protected. She was relieved Eric hadn't seemed to be upset with her that she had invited Kolby to stay with them until they could figure out if anything sinister was truly going on or not at their place.

She didn't want to mention to her brother that two of the deputies staying at the mansion tonight could see ghosts, but she definitely wanted to talk to *them* about it. Just in case they thought the sounds were of a paranormal nature. She didn't want Eric spooked any more than he was already. No way did she want to show Kolby all her abilities at once either. She had to work him up to that. But then she remembered that Mrs. Fitz was supposed to bring pastry treats to them in the morning. She quickly texted her number and told her they were at the Haverton's because of a break-in and would probably have breakfast with them.

Mrs. Fitz texted back: *I'll bring them another day.*

Rosalie texted: *You don't have to.*

I want to.

Okay, thanks!

Rosalie put her phone on the bedside table, glad she'd remembered to tell her, or poor Mrs. Fitz would have arrived to an abandoned mansion!

KOLBY WENT to bed that night, finally, thinking about Rosalie and her ball of light. He suspected that wasn't all she could do. Maybe it was, but it might have been that she was afraid to show him all that she could do and scare him off. He wasn't easily scared off.

He couldn't be more thrilled that she wanted to be his girl-friend! He grabbed his phone off the nightstand and checked the movies at the theater. An animated feature, an adventure thriller, a horror story, and a comedy. He'd go to anything she wanted to.

He realized he didn't even know where she was from. He needed some get-to-know-her time. Maybe he could take her to Jose's Mexican Restaurant.

Then he had a novel idea about Eric and his skill with paint-ing. The Yuma Town library had just been built and they were decorating it now before they had their grand opening. Why not have a local artist paint the murals or framed paintings for the walls? Dottie Barrington was in charge of the project, something she'd wanted to start for the children in Yuma Town. But she'd also wanted it to be a study area for all their homeschoolers and a place for adult readers too.

Not only that, but they were dedicating it to Charity Squire for being Yuma Town's first librarian and historian. They should have Rosalie and Eric cut the ribbon at the grand opening ceremony.

Everyone had contributed money to the project, and they were shooting for a dedication in a couple of weeks. He texted Dottie just to let her know they could have an artist prodigy's paintings to decorate the building. He didn't want to miss out on the opportunity to help Eric earn some more money and for the townspeople to showcase what he had to offer. Oh, and he wanted to be sure and tell her they needed to carry Rosalie's spell caster books too. Wouldn't that be a nice surprise when Rosalie saw her books on a shelf?

He texted Dottie about both and then he realized it was two in the morning. When her message popped up, he hadn't expected her to text him right back.

Dottie texted: *What?*

He smiled and texted: *Sorry for the late text. I just didn't want Eric Squire to miss out on painting for the library if you think it would work.*

Dottie texted: *The snow leopard.*

Kolby texted: *Yeah. He's really a prodigy when it comes to the paintings he creates. I thought you might want to check them out in case you could use any at the library before you get something else.*

Dottie texted: *Does he have a website?*

Kolby texted: *I don't know.*

Dottie texted: *I'll check with him in the morning. And I'll see about ordering Rosalie's books. Night, Kolby.*

Kolby texted: *Thanks, night!*

Now Kolby could go to sleep. But then he couldn't. What about Eric creating paintings for the town center? For Mrs. Fitz's shop? He sent a few more text messages. Then he was finally done, closed his eyes, and woke to a rooster crowing. He rubbed his eyes. He hadn't gotten enough sleep.

When he got up, he wanted to have breakfast at the Havertons with Rosalie and Eric, but he hadn't gotten an invitation. He showered, dressed, and headed into the kitchen to start making breakfast. He was teaching the other ranch hands how to cook, though this morning he was thinking of Rosalie and Eric and didn't bother to wait on the other ranch hands to turn up in the kitchen. It was part of his mentoring of them. Ted would have helped if he was still living at the bunkhouse. Kolby liked making meals with him, but now Ted was staying with his mate at their home and so Kolby was on his own.

He was making ham, hash browns, and scrambled eggs this morning, a nice hearty breakfast for all the ranch hands because of the long workdays they put in. He supposed he should have asked Ted and Hal if it was all right for him to stay with the Squires tonight. While living here, Kolby was responsible for the other ranch hands and the livestock.

The four ranch hands—Curly Renton, Bastian Brookfield, Jasper Holliday, and Timothy Featherston—sauntered into the kitchen. Curly started making the coffee, Bastian was setting the table, and Timothy popped some bread into the toaster. Jasper set out the jam and butter. They were all smiling at Kolby, and he wondered what was up. He suspected they knew that he was interested in dating Rosalie. He wanted to ensure they knew that he was for sure.

Before he could say anything about it, Ted called him. Kolby grabbed his phone and said to the other guys, "Hey, can one of you watch the food and serve it up when it's done?"

"Yeah, sure," they all said. Curly watched the eggs, and Bastian the hashbrowns. Timothy served up the ham. Jasper was pouring mugs of coffee for everyone.

They were really learning to be a team and he really liked all the guys. Curly was the oldest of the new ranch hands at 22 years of age. Timothy was twenty. Bastian was nineteen. Jasper, their resident car thief who had been tried and sentenced here to supervised probation mucking out stalls for four years at the age of sixteen was now eighteen. Jasper had been a royal pain in the ass that first year, but he'd really come around under Ted's tutelage this past year. He'd found a home with them and didn't even want to leave after his final two years were up. He'd graduated from mucking stalls and was helping kids learn how to ride horses, something he'd had to learn how to do also and loved it.

"Yeah, Ted?" Kolby asked.

"I heard through the cougar grapevine that you texted people all night."

Kolby opened his mouth to speak, then closed it. Hell, probably everyone was mad at him.

Ted continued. "Great way to mentor Eric, but it might be better to do it during the day."

Kolby smiled. "Yeah, I just kept thinking of things and couldn't get to sleep last night."

"Everyone could tell."

Kolby chuckled. "I hope I didn't make everyone mad about it. Oh, and I offered to stay with Rosalie and Eric tonight at the mansion to watch for things. I know I should have run it past you and Hal first though."

"No, that works. We need someone to stay there and keep an eye on things for as long as it takes. Since you're mentoring Eric, that works out perfectly. We've got you covered here. And truly, the other ranch hands will take on more responsibility if you're not there to supervise them so much."

"Okay, thanks, Ted. Uh, you didn't happen to hear anything back on whether Chase or Stryker saw or heard anything, did you?"

"Hal said that they heard a bunch of creaking sounds, but it's an old place and they aren't familiar with all the noises it makes. Both Chase and Stryker were wandering around a few times checking things out in the middle of the night. They didn't find anything though."

"Okay. I believe Rosalie and Eric heard something though." Kolby didn't want to dismiss the sister and brother's claim as just phantom sounds.

Curly and Bastian dished up the rest of the food while Timothy served up a plate of toast. Jasper set the mugs of coffee on the dining room table.

"I'm sure they did."

"Nothing ghostly," Kolby said.

"If it had been just Rosalie or Eric that thought they heard someone on the stairs, maybe, but since both of them swear they heard someone, I'd say no, it was someone. Or something. It still might have been a varmint. The place has been vacant for so many years," Ted said.

"Yeah, but how did it get in? I didn't see any place where it would have."

"You would be amazed to see how large an animal can get in through small holes. Even a bear can squeeze in through a car's open window."

"True. But we would have smelled it and we didn't."

"Yeah, that's right. I'm glad you're taking your mentoring Eric to heart."

Kolby was. He was really excited about helping the teen out. And not just because he thought he could make brownie points with Rosalie either. Ted, Hal, and Tracey had helped him and his brother when they needed it, and so he felt that this was just playing it forward. Besides he really liked Eric...and Rosalie.

7

At breakfast that morning with the Havertons and their little ones, Rosalie asked first thing if Chase and Stryker had discovered anything. She was helping to set the table and Eric was keeping the quadruplets—Liam, Tabitha, Denise, and Evan Chase—entertained, to her surprise. She was glad to see him making faces at them and they were making them right back at him. She swore he had changed overnight from the brooding teen to a happy-go-lucky kid again. He'd also let them see Leia and Vader, under his strict supervision.

She hoped he would continue to feel good about being here among the cougars. She was thrilled.

"Since it's already eight, do you want to just stay here for a couple of hours until the other teens arrive, and Eric takes his horseback riding lessons?" Tracey asked. "Eric, and you too, can take a look around the ranch, see the guys working the horse ranch, see all the horses, the new foal, and meet our rambunctious dogs."

"Yeah, sure," Eric said, sounding eager to see everything.

Rosalie hoped it wasn't because he was afraid to return to the mansion. "Yeah, we can do that." Though she really wanted to get back to the place and keep working on it. On the other hand, if she stayed here at the ranch and Eric was more comfortable with it—he had been watching her to see if she agreed—she would do so. She did want to see Kolby in his element here also. Plus, she'd like to see him teaching Eric to ride and how the other teens reacted when they saw him.

Eric looked so grateful that she was going to hang around and she was glad she had said she would.

After breakfast, she helped Tracey clean up while Hal went outside to check on the horses, taking Eric with him. The nanny was cleaning up the kids.

"I hear you were a special agent for the US Fish and Wildlife Service," Rosalie said, impressed that Tracey had worked such a dangerous job.

"I still am. Hal and I go on missions closer to home right now because of the kids."

"That is so cool."

"It's a good job for righting some wrongs and protecting wildlife, but it can be pretty awful too when you find these thugs who kill animals illegally, their smuggling operations, conspiracy, fraud, even money laundering and learn all they're involved in."

"Oh, absolutely. It's great that you both do that."

"Yes, and Ted pretty much has things under control at the horse ranch. On another topic, I hear that your brother loves to paint, and he does a fantastic job at it."

Rosalie smiled. "Yeah, he does."

"I'm redoing the kids' rooms and would love it if he could do something for them. A mural, I think. Eric and I can talk with the kids and come up with something for each of the rooms, if he's interested."

"Wow, okay. That sounds good. I'm sure he will be. I'm going out to check on Eric and the others and see what they're doing."

"Okay, enjoy!"

"Thanks for putting us up for the night and making us a delightful breakfast."

"Oh, you're so welcome. We'll talk again soon."

Then Rosalie went outside and saw Kolby teaching Eric to brush down one of the horses. She smiled. Kolby was so good with her brother. Eric was all smiles, concentrating on the horse. He loved animals.

She hoped it was okay with Eric once Kolby actually stayed overnight with them, but she suspected he would like it if they had an additional cougar in the mansion who could ensure their safety.

Then she joined them, and Kolby smiled at her. "Your brother said you need riding lessons also."

She looked up at the tall horse.

Eric laughed. "You need to, if you're going to date a guy who works with them all the time."

"All right, I'll do it."

"With the homeschool class or do you want a—" Kolby started to say.

Eric interrupted him. "A private lesson for my sister." He smiled broadly.

"Hey," Curly said, "we'll show Eric the new foal."

"Yeah, see? I need to go and see the new foal." Eric headed off with Curly and left Rosalie alone with Kolby.

"This is Sherry. Do you want to ride her? She's very calm. She's a good horse for new riders."

"Yeah, sure." Rosalie wasn't sure she would do well at all. The horse looked so big.

Kolby held the horse's reins while Rosalie climbed into the saddle, and then he walked them around a bit. He finally handed her the reins and climbed onto another horse. "Okay, we'll do this." He talked her through taking charge of the horse and walking her. Then they cantered for a while.

She liked this, though she figured she'd be a little bruised when she finished, but this felt so good out in the chilly air, cantering across the pastureland like she really knew what was doing. She was thinking that she could have a character in her book that rode horses.

That was what she loved about trying out new things because she could use them for her stories and make them different and interesting.

"I heard that Stryker and Chase didn't run into anyone or anything at the mansion," she finally said, feeling comfortable enough to talk while riding.

"I heard the same."

"My brother said he was glad you were staying with us. He did mention the other rooms are full of dust—the bedding and furniture. If you want to stay with me, you can. But if Eric gets spooked, he might join us in his fur coat and sleep at the foot of the bed."

Kolby smiled. "That works for me."

"Okay, good. That's what happened last night, by the way. So I'm serious about him possibly getting spooked and joining me. Or I can clean up all the bedding in one of the other rooms. I plan to, just in case I need rooms that are ready, but I'm still unpacking stuff so it isn't a real priority right now."

"When I go to your place tonight, I can help you unpack and clean anything you need me to also. Staying with you works for me." He gave her a sexy little smile.

She swore whenever he did that, he made her blush. "Oh, okay, thanks."

"I talked to Tracey also about the kitchen appliances. She

had some suggestions, and so did some of the other ladies. Mrs. Fitz also."

"That's good. I sure appreciate everyone's help with this."

"I thought we could order the appliances after I give the teens their riding lessons."

"Did they really have a riding class at ten?"

Kolby's ears turned a little red. "It was as good a time as any other."

She laughed. "Thanks so much for doing this for Eric then."

"Everyone was onboard in an instant," he assured her.

"I love being here."

"I do too. We have a great group of big cats here, and they made all the difference in the world to me. Okay, so I have to ask, what else can you do with your abilities?"

"What if I told you and I scared you off? Or others off?"

"Hell, if you have abilities that are able to pulverize an enemy, I figure you'll be protecting me and Eric tonight."

She laughed. "You're so funny. Okay, I can move things with my mind."

"Telekinesis."

"Right."

"Well, I have to tell you that besides our ghostbusters, we have a couple of people who can tell futures. They see future events. Not for everyone and not all the time, but sometimes."

"Oh, wow, for real?"

"Yeah. You met one of them. Ava."

"Ohmigod, the pastry chef at Mrs. Fitz's shop?" Rosalie couldn't believe it. Which meant Rosalie wasn't as special, or weird, as she thought she was.

"Yep, and her sister, Nina Hill, can also."

"The deputy sheriff who came to the mansion to watch over us."

"Right."

"Did either of them see anything that was going to happen with regard to us last night?"

"No. They would have said so," Kolby said. "Also, Bridget MacKay can read minds. She works here now as one of the special agents for the Cougar Special Forces Division, the CSFD, or frequently referred to as CSF. They're a privately funded organization that helps cougar shifters and cougars and takes down villains who harm either."

"Really. Okay."

"Yeah. She doesn't always try to read people, unless it's necessary to uncover some evil deed. Then she's invaluable. Of course, it doesn't mean she won't catch glimpses of our thoughts. It's just the way it is. So believe me, you'll fit right in. Hell, the rest of us feel like we're not half as gifted."

She smiled. "Believe me, having the gifts can cause more problems than not."

"You don't have to worry about having them around me."

"Thank you."

"On another topic, I was curious about something. When I visited your mansion, I hadn't smelled any cats in the place," he said.

"Oh, Mae came by to offer us a kitten."

Kolby laughed. "That's right. Pookers, as we all call her black cat, had kittens a couple of months ago."

"I think they've been good for Eric since he has been a little unsettled in his room. He keeps them with him."

"Oh, that's good then." Kolby rode with her back to the ranch, helped her to dismount, and then took her in to see the foal. Her brother was busy cleaning out the stalls with another guy. She was impressed. If she'd told him to clean out stalls, forget that. Maybe he could work with the ranch hands a few days a week. She'd have to discuss it with her brother first and see if he was even interested. But he seemed to like all the ranch hands at least.

They heard a couple of cars drive up.

"I guess it's time for me to start teaching the horseback riding class," Kolby said.

"Do they all know how to ride?"

"Some, but it's not something we've done on a regular basis. So we're eager to do it."

"Okay, good." She'd worried that her brother would be a total newbie and everyone else would practically be professional riders and he'd feel insecure about it.

Kolby took charge and started introducing all the teens, including Bobby Mayflower. "Bobby is thirteen, but he was excited to join everyone."

Everyone agreed and Rosalie was glad he was included with the others, and they were eager to have him join them.

Then Kolby talked to the teens about how to handle the horses, how to saddle them, and then they finally went for a ride.

She could tell that some of the kids knew how to ride, but all the kids were so friendly and glad to meet the new teen in town. Eric looked so happy. No one had even asked to see him in his snow leopard coat, but she suspected the other kids' parents had told them not to ask him about it the first time they met him.

She had thought of returning home to get to work on stuff, but she would have to have someone drive her and she thought Eric might still want her here for him. Next time he came, he should be fine on his own. She wasn't worried about being in the mansion alone. Not too much, anyway.

Tracey came out on the front porch and waved to her. "You don't have to stand out there, waiting for your brother to return."

"Oh, okay, thanks."

"Besides, we have a welcoming gift for you and Eric. I was

just getting the basket ready. I had to bake the cookies and fudge."

Rosalie went inside and Tracey showed her the lovely fall basket filled with hot cocoa mixes, cookie and fudge brownies, Yuma Town mugs, and a package of small marshmallows.

"Oh, this is just delightful. Thanks so much."

"We are all just delighted you've taken over the mansion and it's not sitting idly. All our law enforcement guys and gals, including me, took turns making sure no one broke in and looted or vandalized anything, so we're thrilled you're living there now." Tracey began making them mugs of hot cocoa.

"I wondered how it went unscathed for all these years and suspected it was because of your cougar network."

"It sure is."

"Thanks for everything. Both Eric and I love chocolate."

"Hey, our parents told us not to say anything about it," Bobby said to Eric while they were finishing up their riding lessons with Kolby, "but when you feel like it, we want to see you wearing your snow leopard coat. None of us have seen one that is a shifter before."

The other teens looked to see how Eric felt about it. Kolby hoped he wouldn't be bothered by it. The same thing had happened when they learned Ted's mate was a white cougar. No one had seen a white cougar before, not to mention one who was a shifter, and they all had wanted to see her in her white cougar coat.

"Yeah, sure," Eric said.

Kolby was proud of him for saying so. "All right. That sounds good to me. We can run together as shifters after our riding lessons."

"Can you help teach me to drive a car?" Eric asked Kolby. "I've been driving some with my sister."

Kolby laughed.

"I'm turning sixteen in a week."

"A birthday party!" several shouted.

Kolby smiled. "Your sister might have that planned."

"You can both teach me too."

Now that was something Kolby had never planned to do!

"We heard you were going to teach classes on painting, Eric," Sonny said. "I can't wait. We haven't had a real painter teach us how to paint."

"Yeah. I hope it's surreal art though because I can't paint anything that resembles anything," Avery said.

"Me either," her twin brother, Andy, said.

"We'll start out really basic and then work from there," Eric said.

Kolby knew then that Eric was hooked on the idea. Even riding the horse seemed to be second nature to him. He wasn't afraid of the horse and had him under control. He was gentle with him and looked like he'd fit right in here if he wanted to board a horse here and take care of it like some of the kids did. Thankfully, two of the kids had horses boarded here and they hadn't said anything about it, like they needed to learn the ropes too, wanting to set Eric at ease.

Kolby was really proud of all the kids that had shown up for the lessons and had been eager to befriend the new kid in their midst.

8

B ack at the ranch house, Tracey handed a mug of hot cocoa to Rosalie.

"My brother seems to be really happy here and he appears to like the other kids," Rosalie said as they took seats in the breakfast nook.

"I'm so glad. I figured he'd enjoy it."

They drank some of their hot cocoa topped with whipped cream.

"Does your brother have a website showcasing his work?" Tracey asked.

"Uh, yes. He should have some business cards made, but he's been reluctant to do it. Maybe now he will." Rosalie gave Tracey Eric's website: Fantasy World Art.

Tracey immediately checked out the site on her phone. "Oh, these are gorgeous."

Rosalie should just order business cards for Eric, but she knew she needed to let it be his business, not hers.

"Yes, I definitely need him to work on some artwork for the kids' rooms," Tracey said.

Rosalie knew Eric would be thrilled. Maybe he wouldn't

have any time to work at the ranch, but she knew being with others and working with the horses would be good for him too. "I'm sure he'll be happy to do it."

Then someone knocked on the front door and Tracey went to answer it. "Yes, she's here. Okay, Eric. I'd sure love to have you do some artwork in my children's rooms. Can you come and see them before you and your sister leave?"

"Oh, sure." Eric cast a smile in Rosalie's direction.

Yeah, moving to the mansion had been the right thing to do. This had been the best day ever in a long time.

They both went with Tracey to see the kids' bedrooms. A couple of pictures of dragons and dinosaurs were hanging on the walls in the boys' room, while mermaids and unicorns were featured in the girls' bedroom.

Rosalie had no idea what Eric could do with the rooms to impress the kids and the Havertons, but right away, Eric looked at the walls and smiled. "I envision a world of dinosaurs in jungle habitats and dragons flying high above. In the girls' room, an ocean filled with mermaids and fish, the unicorns on an island poking out of the sea, pink clouds and a blue sky overhead. I can sketch them and then let you and the kids approve them. But I think murals would be the way to go."

"That sounds perfect," Tracey said. "I'll drive you home."

"Kolby said he'd drive us home," Eric said.

"Okay, that works," Tracey said.

"Thanks again for the gift basket." Rosalie lifted it off the table.

"Oh, wow, this is for us?" Eric's eyes were huge as he looked over the goodies, but then he took it from her, being chivalrous, and carried it to the door.

"Yes, and we have to share." Rosalie smiled at Tracey. "Growing boy."

Tracey laughed. "I know how that is."

Then Rosalie and Eric left the house and met up with Kolby. She was glad that he was taking them home.

"Are you sure you're going to be all right on your own until I come over tonight?" Kolby asked as they loaded their bags and the kittens into the Jeep, then joined them.

"Yeah, we'll be fine," Rosalie said. "But I imagine it's about time for you to break for lunch and when we get to the mansion, we could fix something before you return to the ranch."

"I can do that. So what do you think about the riding lessons, Eric?" Kolby asked.

"I loved them. And I had fun running in my fur coat with the other kids."

"They loved your snow leopard coat," Kolby said.

"Uh, can I work with the horses too?" Eric asked.

"Yes. We'd love that. I have to warn you though. I told a few people about your artwork, and you might be getting a few orders," Kolby said.

Eric pulled out his phone and scrolled through it. "No emails or text messages or phone calls."

"No, because you don't have a business card and you haven't shared your emails or phone number with anyone. Tracey asked me for your website address, and I gave that to her," Rosalie said.

"Okay, last night before I went to sleep, I ordered the business cards online. They should be in tomorrow."

She sighed. "Good. *Finally*."

Kolby cast her a smile.

"So who else is interested in my artwork?" Eric asked Kolby, sounding eager to get started on a whole lot of paintings.

"Dottie Barrington. She's in charge of setting up the library. It's opening in a couple of weeks."

"Oh, the library? That would be cool. I guess I need to get with her and learn what she is interested in."

"They have a kids' section with books for that age and

another for teens. I wouldn't be surprised if she'd want you to do a mural for the walls in each of those areas. You'll have to talk with Dottie about it. She's in charge of all that stuff and has a whole decorating committee."

"Do you have her phone number?" Eric asked.

Rosalie was proud of him for checking with her right away and not putting it off. She was seeing a whole new side of her brother.

Though she supposed if the library was opening that soon, he'd have to get the painting done at once. Rosalie couldn't imagine doing that on a tight schedule, though she couldn't paint for the life of her, so she knew she wouldn't be able to manage something like that. He could see a scene painted on a wall before he even touched it with a dot of paint, like she could see a scene in her mind when she "painted" her stories.

Kolby parked his Jeep at the mansion where Stryker's deputy sheriff's car was still sitting. Then they got out and Kolby pulled out his phone and gave Dottie's phone number to Eric.

"Hi, this is Eric Squire, the artist," Eric said, grabbing the cat carrier while Kolby got the cat litter box and a bag.

Carrying her bag, Rosalie smiled as she unlocked the door to the mansion.

"Hey," Stryker called out to them. "I was just housesitting until you came home. Chase took off on a call. Hey, Kolby."

"I'm staying with them tonight," Kolby said. "We're having lunch, and then I'm returning to the ranch."

"Will the two of you be all right here alone until Kolby returns to the mansion tonight?" Stryker asked.

"Yes. We'll call you or Kolby, since he's close by if we run into any trouble." Rosalie saw Eric talking on the phone and heading for his art studio. "Did you see any ghosts?" she asked Stryker, her voice low, trying to avoid Eric hearing her.

Stryker looked at Kolby.

"Yeah, I told her. She was worried the place might be haunted."

Rosalie created a ball of light in her hands. "It's okay. I have an unusual ability too."

Stryker stared at the light in her hands, his eyes wide. "Hell, I can't do anything like that."

She smiled. This was the first time she felt special for her ability and not cursed. She felt she could share it with others, just like she wanted them to know they could share their abilities with her, and she was perfectly fine with it.

Eric came out of his art studio, holding onto both kittens. "Hey, I know we were going to just have my birthday party here and eat some ice cream and cake, but that was before I had any friends."

"Oh, absolutely. We could reserve some tables at Mrs. Fitz's shop, or we could—" Rosalie said.

Eric shook his head. "Everyone wants to see this place before the Halloween party. And you know, we gotta to have *your* birthday party during that one."

"Uh, just afterward," Rosalie said, not wanting anyone to feel they had to bring a gift for her. She caught Kolby smiling and nodding at Eric.

She figured Kolby and Eric would do something on the sly anyway.

Rosalie looked at the furniture still covered in plastic.

"We'll get it cleaned up," Eric assured her. "We can order a cake and make this work here. It's in just five days so we have to really move quickly. Come on, sis. We can do it."

Stryker said, "Oh, we changed out all your locks in case anyone has keys to the old locks. Here are the keys. I've got to go into work."

"Thanks so much," Rosalie said.

Then Stryker left, and Kolby asked if he needed to help with making lunch.

"I was just going to make some grilled cheese sandwiches," she said.

"That sounds good," Kolby said.

"She's got this," Eric said.

"COME ON, let's go uncover all the furniture," Eric said to Kolby, all enthusiastic. He set the kittens on the floor to allow them to explore. "At least in the living room and den. Rosalie already cleaned the smaller dining room so we can have the party in there. But I was thinking at my birthday party, we could explore the house first, tell spooky stories, then have a bonfire, roast hotdogs, marshmallows, make s'mores, and play music. Then we could have cake and ice cream in the dining room. Uh, I sent Dottie the link to my website, and she wanted me to start working on a couple of murals for the library right away." He lowered his voice. "I asked her if she could order Rosalie's books and she said you had already mentioned it. She said she has them ordered."

"That's great on both counts. When are you going to do the murals?" Kolby was glad Rosalie and Eric were here now with the cougar town and that they could help celebrate their birthdays. They would love all the birthdays they could attend.

"Dottie gave me a couple of ideas and I'm going to sketch them this afternoon after I help clean some more. I'll need a ride over there to see the new library and give Dottie the sketches. I'll meet with her tomorrow early."

"If you need a ride, just let me know, if Rosalie's busy. We have several drivers at the ranch." Kolby pulled a plastic cover off one of the sofas and folded it on the floor, the kittens quickly pouncing on it.

"Okay, thanks." Eric was pulling the covers off a couple of chairs, then saw what Kolby was doing with them and folded his and added it to Kolby's stack of plastic covers. "Hey, my sister says that girls like it when a guy cooks. Is that true?"

Kolby folded another plastic cover on the growing pile. "They sure do. I'm working with the new ranch hands to teach them how to cook. That makes them self-sufficient and ladies like when the guys can make meals for them too. I can show you some of the meals I like to fix sometime."

"Uh, yeah, sure."

Then they continued to uncover all the furniture. The wood furniture—sideboards, end tables, coffee tables were beautiful oak. They just needed some polishing. The sofas could use some cleaning, reupholstering, or replacing. The wood floors could use some polishing also, and the Turkish rugs needed to be professionally cleaned.

"We'll have you come out to the ranch around your commissioned art jobs and your homeschooling," Kolby said.

"I'd like to earn some money to buy a horse. I mean, I've got money from the inheritance, but you know, Rosalie says I need to save it for my art school fund. If she needs money for the mansion, I want her to have it also."

"When you work at the ranch, you'll be paid," Kolby assured him.

"Oh, great. I'm getting paid for my artwork too."

"That's good. What do you think?" Rosalie asked as she set the plates of grilled cheese sandwiches on the table. Then she returned to the kitchen and brought out a dish with pickles and green olives for whoever wanted them. She gave them glasses of water also, then peeked into the living room. "Oh, my, that's beautiful. It doesn't look half as ghostly now."

"Yeah, I feel better about staying the night here now," Eric said, both he and Kolby washing up, then joining her in the dining room. "I kept feeling like something could be hiding under the covers."

Rosalie laughed. "I did too. I swore sometimes one would move and I'd turn and really look and realize nothing had happened."

"That's creepy," Kolby said, intent on helping them to get this place all fixed up, though he suspected the teens would have liked its ghostly appearance for the party.

They sat down to eat their sandwiches and she ended up making seconds for everyone.

"Okay, we'll need a stack of wood for the bonfire for your birthday party," Kolby said.

"There's a bunch of wood out back of the mansion," Eric said. "I'll text everyone that I want to come."

Kolby hoped he would include Bobby too since he met him at the horseback riding lessons. Bobby really looked up to Eric already.

"You have to show them your artwork too," Rosalie said.

"Yeah, that will be on the tour." Eric smiled.

"Who all are you going to invite?" Kolby asked, grabbing another pickle.

"All the kids at the horseback riding lessons. I guess Jasper could come. He's close to our age, or he might think we're too young for him," Eric said.

"Jasper's eighteen," Kolby explained to Rosalie. "He's a good kid. He'd be a good choice to come to the party. When you come to the ranch, he'll help teach you some of the ropes."

"All right. Then that's who I'll invite," Eric said.

After they ate, Kolby showed Rosalie the different options for appliances for her kitchen and for the new washer and dryer. She chose the ones she wanted and called to order them.

"We'll pick them up for you so you don't have to wait for a delivery date," Kolby said. "They can take forever to deliver out here, which is why we always go pick up stuff."

"Oh, wonderful."

"We've got people who can install everything, including the dishwasher."

"Okay, even better."

Then Kolby coordinated with Ted to have the appliances picked up. "They'll be here this evening, and someone can install them first thing in the morning," he told Rosalie.

"All right. That sounds good."

"A dishwasher, yes!" Eric said. "We need to eat on paper plates until then."

Rosalie chuckled.

"I need to get back to the ranch, unless you think you need me here," Kolby said.

"No, tonight is fine. Thanks," Rosalie said.

"Sure thing." Kolby knew Ted and Hal would be fine if he took off the day to be with Rosalie and Eric because of the scare they had last night. But if they didn't need him during the day, he wanted to be back at work so he could take off a few nights, if he needed to, to stay with Rosalie and her brother. "Don't clean up too much. I'll be back to help you take care of things."

Rosalie laughed. "As if we could clean this whole place up in the next few hours. I'm sure there will be plenty to do. But thank you in any event. You really don't have to help with that."

"I'd be happy to." Now that the kitchen appliances were taken care of, well, almost, but at least ordered and would be picked up today, he wanted to make sure that they did something special for Rosalie for her birthday at the Halloween party. But also, Sheriff Dan Steinacker's birthday was on Halloween, so they could celebrate both. This was going to be so much fun.

He needed to get in touch with Dan's wife, Addie, and coordinate with her too.

Rosalie pulled him into her arms and kissed him. "Thanks for everything. I can't wait to get the appliances in."

Kolby wrapped his arms around her and gave her a heartfelt hug. "I'll be back for dinner, but the appliances will be here before then. If you need anything, and I mean *anything*, even just to talk, call or text me."

"I will."

Then he kissed her, forgetting that Eric was nearby. He released her, saw Eric quickly look at his phone, smiled, and then Kolby said to Eric, "Let me know your schedule and we can work you in on ranch duties."

"All right, will do."

Then Kolby headed outside, hoping Rosalie and Eric would be okay while he was gone. Before the door shut and locked behind him, he heard Eric ask, "Where's the wood cleaner?"

Eric sure had perked up from when Kolby first had seen him. Kolby was glad Eric had met a bunch of kids about his age who could come to his birthday party. They'd be glad to come.

Then Kolby called Addie to talk to her about Dan. "Hey, I know you were thinking about having Dan's birthday celebration before the Halloween party since we're having it at the mansion this year, but Rosalie's birthday is October 31st also."

"Oh, really."

"Yeah, her brother wants to do something for her birthday at the party and I thought we could do something for Dan then too."

"Okay, sure, that would be fun. How spooky is the place?" Addie asked.

"It's fine. We're cleaning it up, except for leaving the spiderwebs on the chandelier and keeping the grungy windows probably, but otherwise, new appliances are replacing the old ones in the kitchen tomorrow, and it's going to be great."

"That sounds like fun. Some of us are coordinating food for the party. Ted did such a great job with scarecrows last year, he and Stella are in charge of those. We'll have to figure out a maze and a haunted house."

"Maybe the guest bedrooms could be used for that. Or there's a big Victorian glassed-in greenhouse that we could decorate for the haunted house."

"All right. I think hanging orange lights up around the mansion, maybe battery-operated candles in the windows would be good. We're making lists."

"Okay, good."

"One of these days, once Rosalie is settled in a bit more, we'll come out and talk to her about it," Addie said.

"She'd appreciate it."

"Dan said you were staying with her for the night."

Word sure got out fast. "Uh, yeah, in case anything else happens at the mansion tonight."

"Good. I was going to send Dan to stay there the night otherwise."

"We've got it covered." Kolby figured between three big cats, they'd be able to tackle anything that might be "haunting" the mansion.

Then they finally ended the call and Kolby arrived at the ranch. The first order of business? He was packing a bag for a few nights' stay. If Rosalie and her brother felt they didn't need him for that long, that was fine, but he wanted to be prepared in case they did.

Ted caught up with him first thing though. Kolby sighed. Ranch business first. Then packing up things to stay with Rosalie and her brother was his next priority.

9

Rosalie was so proud of Eric for finally stepping up to help her clean up the place. She knew the teens probably wouldn't have cared how the mansion looked, but she had to live here, and she wanted it clean.

"I think we should leave the windows all grimy," Eric said.

"Yes! Perfect for the Halloween party." She could live with that as long as their seating areas, kitchen, dining rooms, bathrooms, and their own bedrooms were clean.

"I thought the wood might need refinishing. Maybe the floors, but once we polished up the furniture, it looks great," she said.

Eric agreed.

After about two hours of cleaning and playing with the kittens, they both needed a break and had some deviled eggs, chips, and sodas. "Hey, after we take our break, why don't you go and work on your sketches for the library. If you have time, you could also work on the ones for Tracey's kids."

"Yeah, I was going to ask if it was all right with you if I did that."

"Sure. It's commissioned art, right? So it's a job and you need to get them done."

"Right. I got a request for a painting for the town center also."

"Oh, wow, great!"

"Bobby wants me to do one of wizards, owl familiars, and dragons for his room also, but he has to ask his mom if she can buy it."

Rosalie smiled. "That's wonderful. Kolby wants one for the bunkhouse too."

"Yeah. Here I thought I'd just be painting for my bedroom and the art studio—"

"And me." Rosalie finished her third deviled egg.

"Sure."

"I'm just really happy for you, Eric."

"I shouldn't have ever doubted you about moving to this place."

"We had no idea cougars ran the nearby town."

"Even after we learned that, I didn't realize they'd accept me like they do." Then Eric helped take the dishes into the kitchen. "The dishwasher will be installed tomorrow. Woohoo!"

She laughed. "I'll get these. Go be creative."

"I will. Thanks, sis." Then he took off for his art studio, taking the kittens with him so he could watch them too, and she washed the dishes.

She needed to begin working on some of her current work-in-progress before she forgot what she was writing. But then she heard a big delivery truck pull up and she ran to the front window and peered outside. Three men got out of the truck—ranch hands she remembered seeing at Hal and Tracey's ranch. They opened the back doors of the delivery truck, then hauled out her new stainless-steel fridge. Yes! Her appliances were here. Once they set all of them out of the way in the kitchen and another room and placed the new washer and dryer in the basement, the guy she'd heard was called Curly said, "We'll have a couple of guys install them tomorrow and they'll take the old appliances away to either sell them or give them away for scrap metal. Though we'll change out the fridges now. We could use an extra one in the barn for cold drinks."

"Wonderful. How much do I owe you?" Rosalie asked.

"It's part of your welcome to Yuma Town," Curly said, giving her a wink.

She blushed. As a redhead, she blushed more than she wanted to, that's for sure. "Okay, thanks."

They hauled off the old fridge, hooked up the new one, and then the guys tipped their cowboy hats to her, which she thought was cute, and then they climbed into the delivery truck and headed off for the main road back to the ranch. She put all the groceries from the old fridge into the new one when Eric came to check all the new appliances out.

"Oh, these are so great. Couldn't they have installed the rest of them?" He helped her finish putting the groceries in the fridge.

"Someone else is going to do that tomorrow. We're just lucky they delivered them to us today so we can have everything set up for tomorrow. I have to work on my current book."

"Good luck with that. I'm grabbing a bottle of water, but I had to see our new appliances also."

She thought he should have helped the men, but Eric was wearing splotches of paint on his cheek and hands and so she figured he'd been in the middle of painting a scene and couldn't easily break away from it.

She retreated to her office with a thermos of ice water and another of lavender tea. She sat down at her desk and began working on the story, typing away scene after scene. It suddenly seemed darker in the office, and she hadn't realized how dark it was getting outside.

She got up from her workstation and peered out through the dirty windows. She needed to at least clean her windows! The others were fine for a Halloween party. But she wanted *her* windows to be crystal clear. It was getting late and stormy out on top of that. She needed to fix dinner. Now she wondered what time Kolby would arrive here.

She decided she would make spaghetti and garlic toast. It wouldn't take long, but she texted him to make sure he liked spaghetti and could eat mushrooms, bell peppers, and onions. She was used to making meals for her and Eric, so she needed to remember if she was going to fix food for others, that they liked how she made things!

Kolby called her right back. "Hey, I'm running late. I love everything but peanut butter."

She chuckled. "I won't be putting any peanut butter in the spaghetti."

"Good. I will love it then."

"All right." She smiled. "What time do you think you'll be here? It'll take about half an hour to make the spaghetti."

"I'll be there in about twenty minutes. I'm just packing a couple of bags. I planned to earlier, but Ted put me to work on a project. I finally finished it and will be over there shortly."

"Okay, no rush. Once it's done, it can sit and—"

"Yeah, there's a rush," Eric said, coming into the kitchen to help her cut up the onions and bell peppers. "I'm hungry."

Kolby chuckled. "I'm on my way. I don't want Eric to eat all of it before I get there." Not long after that, Kolby arrived at the mansion and Eric hurried to answer the door.

"It's about time," Eric said.

"I was ten minutes early."

"I know, but I've been starving for a whole hour," Eric said.

Kolby laughed. "I know the feeling. My stomach has been grumbling all the way here."

She figured Kolby got a really good workout at the ranch, unlike what Eric and she got at their sit-down jobs.

Then they took seats in the smaller dining room to eat Rosalie's spaghetti and garlic toast.

"I love your Jeep, by the way," Eric said, glancing under the table. "Leia is tackling my shoelaces. Now Vader is."

"Yeah, I love the Jeep too," Kolby said. "It's a good thing I'm wearing cowboy boots, though I felt some gnawing on one of my boots a moment ago."

Rosalie chuckled.

Eric cleared his throat. "Rosalie made the garlic toast in case we have vampires. We'll be protected." He grabbed a couple of slices of the buttery, garlic seasoned toast.

Kolby smiled. "Vampires, eh?" He took a bite of his spaghetti and nodded. "Now this is good." Then he ate some of the garlic toast. "This is great too."

"I'm so glad you're enjoying them. On another subject, I was thinking if we could replace the broken glass panels in the greenhouse, we could grow vegetables in there," Rosalie said.

"Yeah, that would be a great idea. I was thinking we could use it for a haunted house for the party." Kolby took another bite of his toast.

"Oh, that would be so awesome," Eric said. "We could have spooky music, evil laughter, swinging rats' tails at people when they passed by the garden potting tables, blowing wind, all kinds of neat stuff."

"Okay, we can do that. We'll just need to clean up the glass," Rosalie said.

"We gotta have a skeleton, a skull, smoking potions," Eric said. "Bats."

Rosalie laughed. "Sure, those too."

"Hey, since it's a spell caster's theme, we could have old books and colorful lights coming out of objects, and a black cat," Kolby offered.

"We've never been in charge of a haunted house before. This should be fun." Rosalie ate some more of her spaghetti.

Rain started hitting the windows and she was glad Kolby had made it to the mansion before it started raining so hard.

Lightning speared the ground off in the distance and the flashes of light filled the dining room.

"Now that's what we need for our Halloween party," Eric said. "A good storm like this."

"Hey, that makes me think that we could have lights flashing, and the sound of rain and thunder playing," Kolby said.

"Yeah, that would be great," Eric said.

They hadn't hosted a Halloween party ever and she hadn't taken Eric trick-or-treating since he was a kid of about eleven. He was so excited about all of this, and she was thrilled he was. Not to mention she was delighted about the whole prospect also.

She and Eric usually just watched scary movies, passed out candy to trick-or-treaters, and she made spider deviled eggs and mummy dogs for a meal. Then they ate their favorite Halloween candy for dessert. Hers was chocolate. His was candy corn. This would be so much more fun. The same with Eric's birthday celebration.

"Oh, and if I didn't mention it, I told everyone to bring their fur coats for a run on the wild side after my birthday party. Everyone thought that was funny because we always have our fur coats with us," Eric said.

"I bet they got a kick out of it," Rosalie said.

"We can do that after the Halloween party too," Eric said.

"Yeah. We always do that for all the celebrations." Kolby polished off his third slice of garlic toast.

"Hey, do you want to see the illustrations I did for the library and for the Havertons' kids?" Eric asked Kolby. "After we eat, of course."

"Yeah, I sure do."

Rosalie thought Eric's illustrations were great, but she could never visualize the final painting that would result once he finished them.

"I sent a picture of them in a text to Dottie for the library and to Tracey for her kids' rooms and they loved them. So once I finish the ones in the library first, since there's a quick deadline, I'll do the ones for the Havertons."

"That sounds great," Rosalie said.

They finished up their meals and both Eric and Kolby came in to help her clean up and put the remaining spaghetti away in the fridge.

"That was really delicious," Kolby said.

"Yeah, it was," Eric agreed. "Her spaghetti is really great as leftovers too."

Once everything was cleaned up, Eric led Kolby back to his art studio and Rosalie joined them, wanting to see Kolby's reaction. "Man, these are so good." Kolby was looking over every detail.

"Thanks," Eric said.

Thunder clapped so loud all of a sudden, everyone jumped, and the lights flickered.

"Do you have lanterns somewhere that we can grab if we need them for tonight?" Kolby asked.

Though the big cats had exceptional night vision, it was nice to have extra light if they needed it.

"Yeah, in that box of camping stuff we haven't unpacked yet," Rosalie said, pointing to the box sitting with several others.

Kolby unpacked them. "Do you want to unpack any other boxes? I can help."

"Yeah, sure. A box of linens and towels are over there. We need to grab all the kitchen towels out of them for down here, and the rest go upstairs to the linen closet for the bedrooms."

Kolby sorted through them and pulled out the kitchen towels and set them on the dining table. Then he carried the box of linens upstairs.

"Do you want me to unpack any particular boxes next?" Eric asked her.

"I think we got all our clothes, the rest of the linens, kitchen stuff, your art studio, and my office stuff unpacked. I think the rest of this stuff includes mostly things we don't need right away."

"Okay, then if you don't mind, I'm going to work on painting something."

"Yeah, go ahead." She found another box of cleaning supplies. She thought she'd already unpacked them all. She unloaded a few items for downstairs and then she put the box next to the stairs.

"Is this for me?" Kolby asked, coming down the stairs and pointing to the box at the bottom of them.

She laughed. "I put it by the stairs for when I was going up."

"I'll take it."

"Okay. It's the cleaning supplies for the bathrooms."

He took the box upstairs.

She was thinking she needed to discover when Kolby's birth date was! She needed to get him something special. She grabbed her phone and found his profile on Facebook. November 15th. She smiled and friended him. He was walking from bathroom to bathroom, dropping off supplies, but he suddenly stopped walking and she got a friend request approval from him.

She began opening more boxes and checked to see if there was anything else they needed.

Kolby finally joined her and grabbed up a box of tools and

carried it into the garage. She couldn't have moved that for anything. She'd planned to empty some of the tools out first. She would have had the movers take it out there, but it had been mislabeled.

Then she found files and she could do something with those. She began to unload an armload and took them to her filing cabinet in her office. Kolby found the box she was unloading and carried the whole thing in for her.

She chuckled. "Thanks so much. Those were too heavy for me to move. When the movers brought them, I wasn't too sure where I was going to set up the office or I would have had them use their muscle to put them in here."

"That's understandable. I saw three more boxes of files near that one. Do you want me to bring those in also?"

"Yeah, sure. Thanks."

He lifted it and nearly dropped it.

"What's wrong?"

"Looks like one of your kittens decided to play in it."

She peered inside and saw Vader looking up at her. She laughed.

Then he helped unpack them in her office, giving the empty boxes to the kittens to play in. After another hour of working on the boxes, she said, "Do you want to watch a movie?"

"Yeah, sure. I'd like to take you to one too, as soon as we're both free," Kolby said.

"I'd like that."

"And dinner at Jose's Mexican Restaurant."

"That would be nice." She thought of asking Eric to join them to watch the movie, but when he was in the zone for painting, it was like when she couldn't stop writing on a story. She knew he'd come and join them if he wanted to.

It was still raining and thundering out. She just hoped they wouldn't lose their electricity while they were watching the movie.

She looked at the sofa. "It's...dusty."

Kolby smiled. "Yeah."

She sighed. "Do you mind cleaning some more?"

"Not at all."

"Let me get the vacuum cleaner and one of us can vacuum and the other can shake out the cushions."

"I might be able to shake the cushions out easier." Kolby began gathering the cushions up and Eric came out of his studio.

"What are you both doing?" Eric asked.

"Cleaning cushions so we can sit on the sofa and watch a movie," Rosalie said.

"Okay, I'll help." But before Eric did, he took the kittens up to his room away from the noisy vacuum.

Since moving here and meeting the other cougars, Eric's complete turnaround in his behavior amazed her. She wondered if her brother was trying to impress Kolby. She certainly was impressed.

Then Eric and Kolby took the cushions out on the patio, the patio cover protecting them from the rain while she vacuumed the sofa. She wondered if Eric would join them to watch a movie then. There was enough room for all three to sit on one sofa, but she started working on a chair and another sofa too because they needed the extra seating anyway if any other people wanted to visit.

The guys came in and saw that she had set the other cushions on the floor and was vacuuming a second sofa and chair.

"She's making more work for us," Kolby said.

"Sure, but she's also making enough seats for each of us to sit on so we don't have to crowd each other while watching the movie," Eric said.

She and Kolby smiled. When they were done cleaning the sofas and chair, Kolby and Rosalie cuddled on one of the sofas together, while Eric stretched out on the other sofa. They decided on an adventure thriller—five men and two women trying to find gold in the desert and everyone trying to get it at the same time, greed taking over as soon as they found it.

Once the hero and his party saved the day, it was late and time for bed.

Rosalie realized that Kolby might have needed to go to bed earlier because of having to get up so early at the ranch to do his work. She and Eric could sleep in if they wanted to because their work hours were their own, though she rarely could stay in bed past six. Eric certainly could.

Kolby grabbed his bags and all three climbed up the stairs to the bedrooms. They said their good nights to Eric, and she hoped he wouldn't get spooked tonight and have to join them in her bed. She would welcome him if he did, but she hoped he wouldn't feel the need to on their second night sleeping in the mansion. Eric headed up the stairs to the tower room, closed his door, and locked it.

"I've never had a cougar stay overnight with me," Rosalie admitted to Kolby when they reached her bedroom.

"Since I was human before, I had human girlfriends, and I've dated cougars here, but no one I felt that was meant to be the one for me. With you, I just can't quit thinking about you when we're not together."

"Well, thanks. I have to admit I feel the same way about you, which isn't anything I've ever felt for another cougar, believe me." She opened the drawer to her folded pajamas and night shirts. "I'm going to change in the bathroom and be right out." She loved kissing him, but now that Kolby was actually joining her in bed, she felt a little...shy.

She grabbed a pair of pajamas—orange with a cougar's face

on the shirt wearing a witch's hat—closed the drawer, went into the bathroom, and shut the door. She hoped she wasn't making a mistake with Kolby by sleeping with him this early in their relationship and ruining a good thing. Though if she had wanted him to stay in another room, she should have washed the linens and bedspread already. If she was being honest with herself, she purposefully hadn't washed them for that reason!

When she came out of the bathroom, Kolby was wearing black and orange striped boxer briefs, showing off a beautifully sculpted upper body and legs. His briefs formed a nice package, that she hadn't meant to stare at for so long.

He smiled at her. "I love your cougar."

"I love your boxer briefs. It's good to know you like celebrating Halloween a little early."

"Absolutely. Every occasion in Yuma Town is a cause for celebration."

"I love it here already." She pulled the covers away from the right side of the bed and he pulled the covers away from the left.

"Yeah, when I first came here, it was to rescue my brother. It turned out that we had come just to the right place," Kolby said.

She couldn't help feeling thrilled to be with Kolby tonight. The king size bed seemed so much smaller now that he was going to join her in it though. She was surprised he hadn't been born a cougar. She hadn't met many cougar shifters, but the ones she had met had all been born shifters. He seemed to fit right in. She wasn't sure how she would have handled it if she hadn't been a cougar from birth.

They climbed into bed, pulled the covers over them, and she gravitated toward him. There was no sense in sleeping with him if she wasn't going to get close and personal.

Lightning was still illuminating the room through the heavy curtains and the rain was still pouring down.

Kolby turned to cup her face and began kissing her. This was so nice. She pressed her mouth against his, leisurely enjoying the feel of his warm, vital lips against hers. His hand drifted to her shoulder, and he caressed it. She smiled, wondering just how far he wanted to go. Probably all the way if she was willing. Which she was.

She'd heard wolf shifters couldn't do that. That they had a built-in wolf's need to mate for life so no consummating the relationship until they found the wolf for them. She was glad the big cats could explore sexual relationships before they decided on their forever mate. Though cats didn't mate for life so divorce was a possibility if they ended up with a cougar they decided wasn't the one for them for forever and ever.

Kolby licked her lips, and she pressed her mouth against his again, kissing, licking, her blood heating, her pheromones already getting worked up. She could smell his interest right back as she ran her hand over his torso, his muscles hard, his skin soft.

Then he placed his hand on her breast covered by the soft, flannel pajama top. He gently squeezed and she sighed.

"Too much?" he whispered against her forehead.

"Not enough," she whispered back.

He smiled, a lustful, sexy, I-want-you-too smile. She gave him one back. Then she rubbed her body against his, ramping up the need to have him.

This time he moved his hands underneath her shirt and cupped both breasts, massaging them, rubbing the palms of his hands against her rigid and sensitive nipples. Oh, yes!

He pulled her shirt off and she ran her hands over his nipples, felt them pebble, before he kissed her again, and deepened the kiss.

She slid her hands down to his waistband and tugged at his boxer briefs. She was ready to go all the way with him now, not later. Well, later too. Once she had him, there was no going back. She hoped he realized that.

He slipped his hand down her pajama pants and found her clit and began working it. Ohmigod, he was a dream lover for sure. She moved against his fingers, wanting to climax in the worst way.

He moved his mouth over hers and she circled her arms around his neck, taking his tongue into her mouth, luxuriating with the feel of his tongue stroking hers while his finger was stroking her between her legs.

She didn't want to cry out when he brought her to climax. She was going to bite her tongue, not wanting her brother to hear her making love to the big cat.

But then she couldn't hold back, tensed, felt the end coming, and she was about to cry out with pleasure when Kolby stole her breath, covering her mouth, and kissing her to muffle her cry.

Maybe she should have moved her brother's room even *farther* away from hers!

She was so thankful to Kolby for knowing how she was feeling about her brother being nearby while they were making love. She didn't figure most guys would be that sensitive about it.

She kissed Kolby back and he slid her pajama pants off her legs. She pulled his boxer briefs down his hips, freeing his erection, and he hurried to kick his boxer briefs off the rest of the way.

"Are you ready for this?" Kolby asked in a sincere way, not pressuring her to continue if she wasn't sure about their relationship yet.

"Oh, yeah."

He pushed her legs apart, his mouth and eyes smiling. He looked like he couldn't be any happier. He centered himself between her legs and pressed his arousal in her wet feminine sheath. Yeah, for sure, this wouldn't be a one-time occurrence.

IF ANYONE HAD TOLD Kolby that imagining he had seen a snow leopard running on the ranch would end up in his meeting the snow leopard's cougar sister and making love to her, he would have thought they were living in a fantasy world. But this fantasy was so real. He had never thought he'd ever find a she-cat who intrigued him as much as Rosalie did.

She tightened around him as he pressed into her, and she fit him like a heavenly, wet glove. He slowly pushed in and pulled out, easing into her tight body again. She felt so right, their connection deepening and he knew he wouldn't want to ever let her go. He suspected she felt the same way about him as he did about her.

He began kissing her mouth again, their bodies working together in a poetic rhythm, perfectly synced. He was sure hoping that she wanted him to stay more nights than just this one!

He continued to thrust, her pelvis rising to maximize the pleasure, her hands sliding over his body, pure delight. Their pheromones were all over the place, their musky scent filling him with urgent need. He knew he shouldn't look to the future and want more than what they had right now. This wonderful night with her, enjoying the sex, enjoying being with her. But he couldn't help thinking of wanting more of her like this—sharing meals, watching a fun movie, running with her in their fur coats, making love to her, just everything.

He felt the end coming, held himself still, put off the inevitable, but he couldn't hold back. Not with smelling her sweet scent, feeling her soft body beneath his, seeing her luscious lips parted for another kiss, tasting her lips. Then he was thrusting again, coming, spent, relaxed, and hugging her body.

"I hope—" he started to say.

"It was perfect."

He smiled. "Yeah, I thought so too, but I hope if you wake and want some more loving, you'll feel free to ravish me."

She chuckled. "Your wish is my command."

Then he rolled off her and he pulled her into his arms, not ready to give her up just yet. She was just too huggable.

She seemed to be of the same mind and cuddled against his chest, her hand resting on his belly. Then she sighed. "If you hear anything unusual, wake me and I'll go with you to check it out."

"All right. It's a deal."

He didn't think he'd ever get to sleep while he was enjoying snuggling with Rosalie. But he knew he would have a packed day at the ranch tomorrow and he needed to get his sleep. Then something woke him around two in the morning and he was surprised to realize he'd actually fallen asleep.

What was the sound he'd heard?

Rosalie was still cuddling with him, but she lifted her head, saw that he was awake, and she shifted.

Okay, so she had heard it too. He shifted. They leapt from the bed and headed for the door—the *shut* door. He shifted, opened it, and shifted again. Both of them left the room and stared down the hallway toward the stairs, their ears perked, listening for any further sound.

10

P oor Kolby, Rosalie was thinking. He needed to get his sleep, but she was glad he was joining her to learn what they'd both undoubtedly heard downstairs. She hadn't been sure, but the fact that he was listening for something too had to mean she hadn't dreamed she'd heard something.

They started down the hall, climbed the tower stairs, listened at Eric's bedroom door, but it was quiet, no sounds at all. She figured he was dead to the world after all the work they'd done unpacking and cleaning. Kolby and Rosalie made their way to the curved stairs, then both of them ran down them together. She was glad Kolby didn't feel as though he had to take the lead. Though if there was an intruder with a gun, neither would be safe in their cougar or human forms.

She hoped it was just the creaky old mansion and nothing more sinister than that.

They didn't hear anything going on, no footfalls, no one sneaking around. They peered into the kitchen to see if maybe Eric had gotten up and was in there getting something to eat or drink. But he wasn't. She suspected he was sound asleep in his room still. She should have shifted and checked to see if his bedroom door was still locked. She guessed she was a little fuzzy headed this morning herself.

She and Kolby walked to the basement door and found it wide open. She was sure she had locked it!

Kolby looked at her and she swished her tail back and forth, nervous, irritated. She was ready to call the sheriff's department. Kolby wasn't. He headed down the stairs to the basement like a wary cat, moving slowly, taking a step at a time. If someone had opened the door from the basement, he could be in the house.

She snarled and growled in her cougar cat way, hoping to wake her brother in case she could, and he could at least shift into his snow leopard coat to protect himself better, if they ran into trouble.

Kolby glanced back at her, looking to see why she was making a fuss. She figured he thought she was warning him she'd heard something in the house and not in the basement or was telling him not to go down there any further. Truly, she was at a quandary as to how to proceed.

Maybe Eric had gone down in the basement for some reason at some time yesterday and she hadn't noticed it was unlocked... or that the door was left open. The basement door was out of the way of the main flow of traffic, so it was easy to miss it, if she hadn't specifically checked on it.

Still, she hadn't gone into the basement during the day, so she wouldn't have unlocked it for any reason. Certainly, she hadn't opened the door and left it wide open.

Kolby continued down the stairs and suddenly stopped near the bottom. Rosalie smelled the cold, rainy wind as soon as she walked down a few more steps. That's when she realized the door in the basement was wide open.

Kolby growled low, then checked the entire basement over. Rosalie was with him the whole way. She probably should have been looking around the basement on her own so that they could have taken care of it in half the time. But she wanted to stay with Kolby in case something came out and attacked them.

Then Kolby went to the door and stared out at the rain. She joined him. He shifted and closed and locked the door. "Unless your brother sleepwalks, or you do, someone's been here. Someone who used a lockpick and who wore hunter's conceal-ment spray. I don't smell that anyone was here."

She shifted, shivered, and hugged Kolby. "I don't either."

He hugged her right back, warming her in the chilly air.

Then they both shifted and ran back to the stairs and ascended them. Just then they heard someone coming and saw Eric dressed in his snow leopard coat. He joined them, winding around them in greeting. Kolby shifted and closed and locked the door to the basement.

"Did you go into the basement and leave the door open?" he asked Eric.

Eric shook his furry head. Then Kolby shifted and they explored the whole mansion together to ensure the intruder wasn't in some other part of the place now. They found no one and then headed back upstairs to their own bedrooms.

Rosalie heard her brother's door close and lock. When she and Kolby reached her room, they shifted, and he closed the door, then they got into bed.

She let out her breath on a heavy sigh. "What do you think?"

"If you or Eric didn't do it, or either one of you hadn't forgotten you had, I'd say that we've had an intruder visit again. Unless Eric was afraid to admit he had left the basement doors open."

Rosalie shook her head. "Since this is a really serious issue, I don't believe he wouldn't admit to having done that. What about the security cameras?" Rosalie wondered if when they were installed, they'd catch the person doing this.

"They're being installed tomorrow. We'll catch whoever it is on camera at the very least if he comes again."

"Okay. I wonder if he came into the house. I mean, he wouldn't have come into the basement and unlocked the basement door to the house and not come inside, I don't believe." Which gave her goosebumps just thinking about it.

"I agree. I suspect he, or she, comes when you've gone to sleep though, not during the day."

"But why?"

"To get out of the cold, to sleep. There's an old mattress on a bedframe down there, and he might be sleeping there during the night. The mansion has been abandoned for so long, I wouldn't be surprised if he thinks he can live here if he wants, if he's been here for a while. We'll just have to catch him at it and learn what the deal is. He can't stay here like this. We don't have any idea who he is or how dangerous he could be. The fact we changed out all the locks and he got in anyway means he must be using lockpicks, and not one of the original keys to the house."

"Or it's a ghost." She didn't believe in them, but what if?

Kolby chuckled, making her feel better about it. "I believe it's someone very real."

At least if it was someone real, they could catch him at it. But that was a scary idea too.

"I'll talk to Dan about having a security detail in the basement at night. During the day too, if it appears to be necessary."

"Okay, I think that's a good idea for at night at least, until we know what we're dealing with."

He kissed her lips. "Yeah."

Then she began to kiss him too. And they were back to making love. So something good had come of them having to get up in the middle of the night for the disturbance.

Later that night, their sleep was disturbed again, only this time when they shifted and investigated the basement, the basement door was still locked, both upstairs and downstairs. She was glad for that. They also checked over the whole house and didn't find anything.

She figured it was just a creaky place and she'd have to get used to it. Except she knew the earlier sound had to have been from the intruder because of both doors being left open. Which meant? He had probably left in a hurry.

THE NEXT MORNING the rain had stopped, and Kolby was in a rush to get a shower and head to the ranch to work. He glanced back at Rosalie lying on the mattress, the sheets draped over her body, making her look like a siren. Her eyes were sparkling in the lamplight, her lips curved up as she watched him. He wanted to go right back to bed and make love to her again. Twice wasn't enough. But he had to get to work.

She sighed. "I'll peel myself out of bed and make you breakfast."

"You don't have to."

"Yeah, I do. You need a hearty breakfast before you go to work." She slipped out from under the covers, beautifully naked, and then pulled on her pajamas, a pair of slippers, and a robe.

He came over and kissed her again. "I'll be down in a minute."

"All right. See you soon."

He went into the shower and took a quick one, the pipes groaning and creaking a bit.

When he dressed and headed down the hallway, he figured Eric was still sound asleep. Kolby descended the stairs and joined Rosalie in the kitchen, wrapping his arms around her, and kissing her neck.

"Hmm, too bad you have to go to work. Eric is still sound asleep."

Kolby chuckled. "I would like nothing better than to return to bed with you."

"Oh, I meant for you to help me with cleaning."

He laughed. "Sure you did."

She smiled. "You're—ack, need to watch my cooking." She quickly served up the hash browns, while he took care of the sausages. "Toast is coming right up."

"I've got the eggs."

Then she poured them both some coffee and added milk and sugar to hers.

"Same for me," he said. "What about Eric?"

"He grabs something when he finally gets up. Sometimes that's at ten. Sometimes he just has lunch with me by the time he wakes and showers."

"Hmm." Kolby forked a sausage. "If he wants to work on the ranch, he'll have to get up as early as the rest of us."

She smiled. "While you're staying here with us, you can roust him out of bed and take him with you."

Kolby laughed. "I bet that's not easy."

"Nope, but he might do it for you. He really wants to impress you."

"I've noticed. He's a good kid." Then they finished their breakfast and Kolby kissed her goodbye, glad she said he was staying with them for longer. "I'll be back for dinner. Leftover spaghetti works for me."

"Oh, we'll have that for lunch. I'll fix us salmon and mixed vegetables tonight, if that works for you."

"Yep, it sure does."

"We'll have all new appliances installed by the time you get here."

"I can't wait to see them." It would really spruce up the

kitchen, though he was thinking they needed to update it further: get rid of the old backsplash, create an island with storage underneath, redo the floral wallpaper, and install granite counters, if that worked for Rosalie.

"Me either."

Then he walked out to his Jeep, waved goodbye, and headed out to the main road. One of these days, he needed to get a new Jeep. But he was thinking he might just overhaul this one and give it to Eric for his birthday. It would be great for Eric to use to learn to drive, if he and Rosalie were agreeable. Until Kolby got a replacement for his Jeep, he'd just use one of the ranch pickups to get around.

He finally drove onto the ranch, parked, and started checking to see if everyone was up and working. All the ranch hands were, to his surprise. He was glad for it, to know that he could be away, and the jobs were still getting done.

"Any more spooks?" Ted asked, joining him as Kolby checked on the foal.

"Yeah. I had hoped we all had scared whatever it was away, but both the doors to the basement that led to the house and to the outside were wide open in the middle of the night," Kolby said.

"That's not good, and no one left them open by accident, I take it."

"Neither Rosalie nor Eric remembered doing so."

"Are you going to stay there a while longer? At night, I mean," Ted asked.

"Yeah, if it's not a problem."

"Nope. You can see that everything is getting done just like it should be."

Kolby suspected Ted had made sure of it in his absence. Kolby had taken on more of the role because Ted was known to stay in bed a little while longer with Stella now that he was mated. After spending the night with Rosalie, Kolby knew just how Ted felt. Though tonight, Kolby planned to go to bed a little earlier. He hoped Rosalie would want to come with him. After making love to her twice in the night and then checking out the mansion a couple of times in his cougar coat, he felt he needed a nap. But perks on the ranch didn't mean they got naptime for cowboys.

"You look like you didn't get enough sleep last night," Ted said.

Kolby smiled at him.

"I thought maybe you had problems last night," Ted continued.

"Rosalie and I did prowl around the house twice last night in our cougar coats, when we thought we heard strange noises. The second time we heard something, there wasn't anything going on." Kolby suspected Ted wanted to know if he stayed with Rosalie the night and if that's why he didn't get enough sleep, but he didn't kiss and tell. "I called Dan on the way over here to see about him posting a deputy overnight for a few nights to catch whoever it is."

"That doesn't sound good about the doors being wide open. I'm glad the sheriff's department will start watching over the situation."

Then they heard Ricky's deputy sheriff's SUV pull up and Kolby wondered what his brother was doing here. Ted would have told Kolby right away if they'd called the sheriff's department because they'd had some trouble this morning.

"Hey, Ricky," Ted said to him as he got out of his vehicle.

Kolby swore his little brother had a swagger when he wore his uniform. Ricky swore Kolby did when he was all decked out in his Stetson and the rest of his cowboy gear. "Morning, Ricky."

"I heard you stayed at the mansion last night," Ricky said, shutting his door.

"Yeah."

"I heard you had issues at the mansion again," Ricky said.

"Yeah, but whoever it was wasn't there when we checked," Kolby said.

"You should have called me. Dan told me about it, and I'll be pulling duty there tonight. I want to catch this guy."

"Oh, great. You'll have dinner with us then?" Kolby asked.

"Nah, I'll have dinner with Mandy and the little ones first and then I'll be right over. At eight months old, Cameron and Skye are a lot to handle at mealtimes."

"Sure, that works. Does Rosalie know you'll be staying with us?"

"Yeah, Dan told her already."

"Okay, that'll be perfect." Kolby was thinking he needed to set up things for Ricky so he'd be more comfortable in the basement for the night. Sure, Ricky would be awake, watching for any sign of anyone coming into the place, but he still could be comfortable while he was pulling security detail.

"I was just patrolling in this area, so I wanted to tell you I'd be over, but Chase is dropping me off at the mansion tonight. We don't want a deputy sheriff's vehicle parked out in front of the mansion."

"Good thinking. Okay, we'll see you tonight, brother."

"See you." Then Ricky got back in his car and drove off the ranch.

Kolby called Rosalie. "Hey, my brother, Ricky, who is a deputy sheriff, just dropped by and said he is staying in your basement tonight. He'll be having dinner with his mate. After that, Chase will drop him off at your place. I figure I'll set things up down there so he's more comfortable for the night. Well, for all the deputies who pull duty in the basement over the next few nights."

"Eric and I are on it. We're setting up a small fridge down

there that Eric just bought to keep some cold drinks in his art studio. We've cleaned up the basement bathroom. We carried a chair down there and put fresh bedding on the mattress. I know Ricky won't be sleeping, but he can lie down if he needs to stretch out. At least the basement isn't moldy."

"Okay, I was going to help you with that. If there's anything else you need assistance with, just let me know." He didn't think the two of them should be lifting small fridges and carrying them down the stairs.

"Thanks. We'll see you later. Oh, and the guys have arrived to put the appliances in! I can't wait to see how it all looks or works."

"Send me photos when they're done."

"I'll do that. Some others are setting up motion-activated lights outside and security cameras also."

"That's good to know."

"I'll see you tonight," Rosalie said.

"See you." Then Kolby joined Ted and the other men to learn what else needed to be done this morning at the ranch.

Hal soon joined them, and Kolby said, "What do you think about putting in a gravel road to the fence that runs past the mansion, and put in a cattleguard and walking path next to it so we can run as cougars or walk there?"

Hal smiled. "I was just talking to Tracey about that this morning."

"We figure we can get to Rosalie and Eric's place faster and he can drive on the road between our places without any supervision after he's had a number of driving lessons and we're sure he'll be good to drive there," Kolby said.

"Yeah, you don't have to convince me or Tracey. Oh, and I'll be staying tomorrow night at the mansion."

"Okay, we're fixing it up so you'll be more comfortable staying in the basement."

"We appreciate it," Hal said. "We're having graders come out this morning to work on the road. We have that old wagon trail out there, so we'll be using that one for the road."

"That sounds great." Kolby was glad he didn't have to convince them to do it. But then he wondered if they were doing it because they figured Kolby was going to end up mating Rosalie and *he* could reach the ranch more quickly. He smiled. He'd thought of that too.

Then he got to work. He loved working here and enjoyed being with the other cougars at the ranch, but he couldn't wait to see Rosalie again tonight. She was an obsession he wanted to feed.

11

That night after seeing all the new kitchen appliances, then checking out the security cameras and motion detectors, Eric, Rosalie, and Kolby made salmon, potatoes, and spinach for dinner. After they ate, Eric gratefully loaded the dirty dishes in the new dishwasher. When Ricky showed up to begin his basement watch, Kolby introduced Ricky to Rosalie while Eric went to play with the kittens in the living room.

Kolby knew Rosalie had seen Ricky before, but they had been cougars at the time, and Kolby hadn't been able to introduce her to him back then. Ricky gave Rosalie a hug. "I'll try and catch whoever the intruder is."

Rosalie hoped he would, but that he wouldn't get hurt in the process. "At least we have security cameras now, and Dan had some men install motion detectors too."

"All that should help. If not to catch him, maybe to deter him. Hal will be here tomorrow night," Ricky assured them, "if we don't get him tonight."

"I'll visit with you for a while," Kolby said to his brother.

She thought that was nice of him.

"You don't have to. I'm just doing my job." Ricky glanced at Rosalie as if he knew Kolby would rather be with her.

"I'll be up in a while to join you," Kolby said to Rosalie.

"I'll keep her company," Eric said, as if she needed anyone's company.

She wanted to laugh. She would just write on her story for a while.

When the brothers went down into the basement, she said to Eric, "I'll just write unless you want to watch something on TV with me."

"Yeah, I'll see a movie with you."

"Okay, sure." Eric normally didn't, so she was surprised he'd want to watch something with her for a second night in a row.

"Do you think Ricky will get whoever it is?" Eric asked and to her surprise he brought out the business cards he'd ordered. "I almost forgot to show them to you."

"Oh, they're beautiful," Rosalie said, looking at the fantasy fae, elf, and wolf scene he had painted in an enchanted forest.

"Thanks."

"As to your question if Ricky will get whoever it is, I don't know. If the intruder sees the security cameras or had watched as they were being set up, or even saw Chase dropping off Ricky in the deputy sheriff's vehicle, he or she may stay away."

"Oh." Eric stretched out on the sofa he'd used last night, the kittens playing in a box nearby. "That's not good."

"Well, if he stays away, that's okay, but if he doesn't, then no." She curled up on the other sofa and they selected a movie to watch. A nice paranormal thriller. Though she wished she was watching it while she was snuggled up with Kolby.

∽

Kolby and Ricky sat down on the mattress in the basement, not saying anything at first, listening to the TV on upstairs. It sounded like a thriller. Kolby smiled, wishing he was with Rosalie watching it. But he'd be with her tonight at least.

"So, how are you getting along with Rosalie?" Ricky asked.

Kolby knew that's what his brother had wanted to ask him at Hal's ranch, but maybe not in front of Ted. "Good."

Ricky smiled. "I was worried that you would never find a she-cat for yourself."

"Yeah. I'd had that thought too." Not that Rosalie and Kolby had decided to mate or anything.

"So what do you think's going on here?" Ricky asked.

"I think it has to be a shifter. I might be wrong, but I don't think it would be a cougar. I'm sure he, if it's a he, would make himself known."

"So a wolf or a bear then."

"Or a caracal. We've had that family here too."

"Ahh, I'd forgotten about them," Ricky said.

"Yeah, though I can't imagine the caracal family sneaking into the place and not letting us know it's just them," Kolby said.

"I agree." Ricky turned to Kolby and smiled. "Hey, enough chitchat with me. Go join Rosalie. She'd make a great sister-in-law."

Kolby smiled. "Okay, let us know if anything happens in the basement. I'll be down here in a heartbeat."

"All right. Enjoy your night."

"Stay safe." Kolby was used to protecting his younger brother, so it was hard to give up that role now that he was full grown, married even, and a deputy sheriff.

"I will," Ricky said.

Then Kolby headed upstairs to join Rosalie and Eric in watching the movie, the kittens curled up on his lap. Kolby sat on the sofa and pulled Rosalie into his arms. Perfect. He was doing the job he wanted to do, taking care of Rosalie, and Eric, of course.

After the movie, they headed to their beds and Kolby texted his brother. "We're headed to bed, Ricky. If anything happens, get hold of me."

"Will do."

Kolby just hoped he would if he got into any trouble. They said good night to Eric and continued down the hallway to Rosalie's bedroom.

"Is Ricky going to be all right on his own?" Rosalie asked, pulling Kolby into a hug in her bedroom.

"Yeah. He'll let me know if he needs help."

"Okay, I just don't want him to get hurt."

"Me either. He'll be fine. I'll check on him in a couple of hours."

"Good." Then she started to undress Kolby, and he smiled and helped her out of her clothes. First things first.

A COUPLE OF HOURS LATER, Kolby woke. He checked his phone, but Ricky hadn't texted him. Kolby sat up in bed and Rosalie looked at him. "Is there something wrong?" she asked.

"No. Ricky didn't text me about anything, but just to be sure, I'm going down to check on him."

"I'll come with you."

"Sure." Kolby left the bed and went to the door and opened it. Then he shifted and she did also, and the two of them went down the hall to the stairs. They ran down the stairs together and went to the basement door.

Kolby shifted and opened the door, shifted again, then he ran down the stairs and Rosalie followed him. Ricky was sitting on the chair with his phone in his hand when he saw them running down the stairs as cougars to see him.

Ricky smiled. "Nothing has happened yet. The two of you should be sleeping soundly. I'm all right. There's not been a peep in the least."

Kolby shifted. "I'm afraid he's been spooked."

"We'll keep someone here at nights for a while. He might have decided there was just too much activity for him to return," Ricky said.

"Okay, we're headed back to bed then."

"Good. I'm watching a great show on my cell."

Kolby shifted, then he and Rosalie returned to bed. They were so tired, though they still made love a second time. When the dawn came, Kolby was surprised he hadn't awakened at some point to check on his brother again.

He smelled bacon and eggs, and he realized Ricky was making them breakfast. Or maybe Eric was, though Kolby suspected he wouldn't be up yet.

He looked over at Rosalie. She was still sound asleep. He kissed her cheek. He knew he loved her already. He wanted this to be the way it was for them always—minus intruders and having to have deputy sheriffs staying the night to watch over them.

He hurried to get dressed and Rosalie woke, looked at him with half shut eyes, ran her hands through her hair, and groaned. He came over and kissed her again. "Hey, sleepyhead. Someone's fixing breakfast. You don't have to see me off. You're worn out."

She sighed, then took a deep breath. "Who's making breakfast?"

"Ricky or Eric, I figure."

She got out of bed and gave Kolby a hug. "Let's go join them." She hurried to get dressed and brush out her hair.

"Does Eric cook?" Kolby asked.

"Oh, yeah. I taught him when he was young. I believe in being self-sufficient and I wanted him to be able to prepare his own meals if I wasn't around to cook them for him."

"That's wise."

"But I also told him girls love it when a guy can cook, which he didn't really believe. I suspect he's still sleeping though," Rosalie said.

Kolby smiled. "He's coming around on the idea for cooking for girls."

Rosalie laughed. "Good."

Once they were fully dressed, they headed downstairs to the kitchen and found Ricky cooking the breakfast. That's what Kolby had suspected. "Morning. Thanks for making breakfast."

"You're welcome. I figured you'd need to get into work early and since no one was up, I'd start breakfast. I thought Eric was supposed to begin working at the ranch part time."

"Once he's finished some of the paintings he has orders for, and then I've got to start taking him in early with me to work for a few hours," Kolby said.

"That's going to be a feat," Rosalie said, "unless we can get him to bed earlier at night."

"Well, at least I was able to report back to Dan that we didn't have any unwelcome visitors last night. He was glad in a way, but he also wanted to know for certain who has been breaking in," Ricky said.

They heard someone coming down the stairs and saw Eric carrying the kittens, looking tired. "I'm awake. I'll go with you this morning to the ranch," Eric said, setting the kittens on the floor, then rubbed his eyes. "Since I got up early enough to catch a ride. I have to be at the library painting all afternoon after lunch though."

"Yeah, sure thing." Kolby helped set the table while Ricky

dished out the food and Eric got everyone glasses of orange juice.

Rosalie set mugs of coffee on the table. Then they all sat down to eat.

"You'll need some proper clothes for the job. We'll loan you some things," Kolby said to Eric. But he was thinking that would make great birthday gifts too.

Rosalie looked at him and he suspected she was either thinking the same thing or maybe she had gotten some for Eric already.

"Are you going to be all right by yourself?" Kolby asked Rosalie.

"Yeah, I'll be fine," Rosalie said. "No problem at all. If anything happens at all, I'll be calling right away."

"I can stay for the day and sleep on one of your sofas," Ricky said, as he and everyone else finished off their breakfast.

"No really, I'll be fine."

"All right," Kolby said. They started getting ready to leave.

Ricky and Eric told her goodbye and then they went out to the Jeep so Rosalie and Kolby could have a moment alone. "I got Eric some clothes for working on the ranch for his birthday," Rosalie said.

"I figured that's what that look was all about. I'll loan him some things if he needs anything."

"Okay, thanks."

"If you see anything at all that's a problem, just give me a call right away."

"I will. I promise," she said.

Then he kissed her, and she kissed him back. Dinnertime wouldn't come soon enough.

12

Rosalie cleaned up the dishes from breakfast and was kind of glad to have the day to herself. Eric was practically with her all the time, even if he was in his bedroom half the time, and now in his own art studio. She almost felt like an empty nester. She was so glad Eric wanted to work at the ranch. It was so good for him to be around other guys who could act as big brothers to him.

She carried the kittens into the large cordoned off area in one of the meeting rooms Eric had created so that they didn't lose them in the huge mansion while they were working or having people in and out of the place. She couldn't believe what a nice job of it that Eric had done. Water dishes, food dishes, cardboard boxes and a paper sack, little cat beds, though they slept together, and drank and ate from the same dish, the climbing tower, blankets to curl up on, or slip underneath, litter boxes, and their toys were all laid out in their "room."

She ascended the stairs to the second floor and walked down the hall to a door that led to stairs in the attic. She paused, hoping it wouldn't be full of spiderwebs and creepy crawly things. After opening the door, she saw that the attic actually had a light switch. Great! She turned on the light and headed up the stairs, creaking with her every footfall. When she reached the attic room, she found a steamer and a humpback trunk. So cool. An antique wrought iron crib sat in one corner of the expansive room, and light filtered in through the dirty dormer windows, showing off all the dust floating in the air.

She hurried over to one of the trunks and lifted the lid. Inside, she found antique hat boxes and other vintage wear. Lace gowns, Victorian hats. She might even be able to use some of this for later parties. Then she found a velvet box of jewelry— a pearl necklace, pearl clip-on earrings, and emerald necklace and bracelet, but then she saw a gold locket and pulled it out of the box. When she opened it up, she saw a picture of a young man and woman, most likely Max and Charity.

Rosalie slipped the necklace over her head and set the jewelry box aside. Then she discovered another box, this one filled with photos. In the steamer, she saw tons of antique clothes. Again, she thought they could be fun for dress up.

She took both the box of photos and the jewelry downstairs, then closed the door to the attic stairs.

Once she reached the first floor, she went to one of the dining room tables in the smaller of the two dining rooms and spread out the photos. On the back of each, dates and people's names were recorded, which sure helped! Even her dad's photo was there when he was a baby with his mom and dad. She was sad to see him and missed him. But she was also sad that Eric didn't have any early photos of his parents. Though she didn't have any of her mom either.

She glanced at the wall clock and realized if she didn't get to work, she wasn't going to get anything done. She went into the kitchen, made Earl Grey tea and filled a thermos, then filled another with ice and water, took them into her office, and sat down to write. Today would be a productive writing day. She just knew it.

Then she got to work on her writing. Later, she would wrap Eric's birthday presents. Her doorbell rang and she looked at her phone. Good. A delivery.

She hurried off to the front door and found the packages she'd been waiting for. Blue balloons, water balloons, streamers, party favors for all the kids—invisible ink, waterproof pens, notepads, packages of chocolate candy, and party-favor canvas bags.

She put all the items in the living room on the coffee table. Eric could help her put the bags together for the other teens. She'd do it, but she knew he'd like to be involved, since he'd picked out the party favors for the others.

"Oh, no." She'd forgotten all about ordering a cake for her brother's birthday. She called Mrs. Fitz and asked if she could place an order for a cake for her brother for his sixteen-year-old birthday party.

"Absolutely. I'll let you talk to Ava about the particulars. Oh, and because you're back at the mansion, I'll bring the pastries for breakfast, but I'll add one for Hal—his favorite, since I hear he'll be on security duty over there—and Kolby."

"You really don't have to."

"I want to."

"Okay, thanks." Then Ava got on the line, and Rosalie said, "I need to order a chocolate birthday cake for my brother who will be sixteen tomorrow. I should have ordered it earlier"—she felt bad that she hadn't remembered to do it before this—"but things have been rather hectic around here. If you can't make one in time, I'll understand."

"It's no trouble at all. May I make a suggestion?" Ava asked.

"Oh, absolutely."

Ava was the pastry chef after all. "We could make the cake into a 1950s Chevrolet Impala with a big license plate and car keys."

"Ohmigod, that would be too cute."

"Do you think that would be okay for him? Or do you think he'd like a pickup truck better?" Ava asked.

"How about a Jeep? Eric loves Kolby's Jeep," Rosalie said.

"A Jeep it is. What time do you need it by?"

"The party's at six, so can I pick it up before then?"

"Sure, or one of the moms who is dropping off some of the teens for the birthday party can bring it to you. That'll save you a trip."

"Oh, thanks so much. If it wasn't that I've had so much going on—" Rosalie really was embarrassed that she'd waited so long and had nearly forgotten it.

"I know. Especially with the intruder bothering you."

"Yeah, that's been nerve wracking."

"I don't think you'll have much trouble with him. He seems nice enough. If it's him."

"What?" Rosalie was stunned by Ava's comment. Had Ava known all along who it was and was keeping it secret for some reason–until now because she'd slipped up?

Dead silence. "Oh, God, I'm so sorry. I guess I had a premonition about it. It happens sometimes and they just pop into my head. Uhm, yeah, I sense the man wants to speak with Eric."

"Who is he?" Chill bumps raced up Rosalie's spine.

"I don't know. Only that he wants to talk to Eric."

"Is he human? A shifter?"

"I don't know. Sorry. I just see him at your front door asking you if he can speak with Eric."

"Can you see his face?" Rosalie had to know who he was.

"No. He's tall and dark haired, broad-shouldered, wearing a shirt, jeans, hiking boots, and a lightweight, black jacket. Nothing that gives me any indication of who he is or where he's from."

Rosalie thought it was less scary knowing the man just wanted to speak to Eric, though why, she couldn't fathom. "Why has he been coming to the mansion and breaking into the basement then, if he just wanted to speak with my brother?"

"That I don't know. All I know is the man knocks on your front door and you answer it. I don't know if Kolby is there with you, or you allow this guy to speak to Eric, or even if Eric is at the mansion at the time. I can't tell the season, like if it's fall or winter, summer, spring. All I see is him at your door and you open it to him."

"Do I think it's a delivery man?"

"I don't know. I would just be cautious of opening the door to anyone."

"Okay, thanks." Rosalie needed to look out the windows and not just assume whoever had arrived was helping to install or deliver something. She'd had so many deliveries or men over there to help her out, she was getting lax.

"I'll let Nina know about what I've seen. Sometimes my sister will have a different premonition that is more detailed about the same event than I have, or vice versa. She'll call you. Since she's a deputy sheriff, she'll tell Dan and the rest of them who work with her about it," Ava said.

"Okay, thanks." God, what could this be about?

"In the meantime, I'm off to make a Jeep cake. Oh, what color would you like it to be?"

"Light blue. That's Eric's favorite color."

"You got it."

"Thanks." Then Rosalie went into her office and got online

to pay for the cake. After that, she called Kolby, "Hey, I just spoke to Ava. I'd forgotten to order Eric's birthday cake. Ava had a vision regarding who the intruder is. She's going to speak to her sister to see if she had a vision too. Nina will let me know if she has any about the intruder. Also, Nina will pass the information on to the other deputy sheriffs and Dan."

Kolby listened while Rosalie told him the rest of what had been said, then he said, "Okay, so who do you know from your past who looks like that who would want to talk to Eric?"

"Nobody. Eric didn't attend school in Loveland. He home-schooled, so he wouldn't have anyone looking for him who'd been a friend or teacher. Eric didn't really have friends there. He isolated himself from everyone but me, mostly because of us being shifters."

"You don't have any family left?"

"Uh, his father, but he left Eric's mother before Eric was born and moved back to Alaska where he was from. He's never had any contact with Eric."

"But Eric's nearly sixteen."

"I know that!" Rosalie couldn't help being angered by it. If Eric's father was showing up now because he learned Eric's mother and stepfather had died nearly six years ago, or because he knew but he hadn't wanted to raise a ten-year-old on his own —well, he just better not plan to take Eric away from here. Though she didn't know if the intruder was him at all, so she shouldn't be borrowing trouble.

"If it is his father—" Kolby said.

She ground her teeth.

"Then Eric needs to speak with him, if he wants to, but we need to be there in case he tries to take him with him back to Alaska? Right?"

"Yeah." God, what if Eric wanted to go with his dad and get

to know him and do all the fun stuff a teen could do up there. Hunt? Fish? Hike? See all the sights in the wilderness? Polar bears? Eric could have a ball up there.

She let out her breath on a heavy sigh. She had to think of Eric and what he really wanted to do. What if he went with his dad just to see the place and visit with him for a bit, but when he planned to return home, his dad wouldn't let him go? He was still his dad. She was just his grown stepsister.

Though she had looked into adopting him right from the outset. The problem had been that she had needed to locate his father to obtain his consent to forfeit his son so she could adopt Eric. Without that, she couldn't do it. So they had just lived as siblings, and she had raised him.

On the other hand, if Eric wanted to get to know his father and maybe even meet more snow leopards like himself if there were any up there still, then she had to let him leave. It would kill her though. She wasn't ready to let him go.

"Okay, well, we'll work things out one way or another, Rosalie, darling. Don't stress over it. Ava didn't have any idea when the guy would actually knock on your door, so it could be a month from now."

"Or tomorrow, when we celebrate Eric's birthday."

"I'll be there with you all day."

"Are you sure Ted can afford to miss you?"

"Yeah. I already talked to Hal and Ted about this situation if it seemed the guy isn't going to give up on sneaking into your mansion. With this new news, I'm staying until he comes. One thing that Ava might not have said because she doesn't want to assure someone when her visions will actually come to pass, but they usually occur fairly soon after she's had them. It wouldn't be spring, summer, winter even. More likely it'll be sometime in the next few weeks."

Rosalie was betting on tomorrow—Eric's birthday.

"I can come home now if you need me too."

"No, that's okay. I'm going to get back to work on my story."

"All right. If anyone comes to the door, let me know at once. Don't answer it unless it's someone you know."

She smiled. "I won't."

"I'll try to be home early for dinner."

Boy, if that didn't sound like he lived here already. And she loved the notion. Then she got back to work on her story, glad Kolby and the others were in her and Eric's lives now. When it was finally time for lunch, she wondered if Eric was coming home for lunch or staying at the ranch and having it with the guys.

She figured she should tell him what Ava had told her and just mention there was a possibility the guy might be his father. But she really wanted to speak to him in person about it.

Just then Eric called her, surprising her. "Hey, sis, the guys asked if I'd stay for lunch. Is it all right with you?"

"Oh, yeah, for sure." She was so glad he was enjoying his time being with them. "I'm just going to have a tuna fish sandwich, nothing special."

"We're grilling hamburgers. Kolby's even showing me how to do it. Do you want to join us?" Eric sounded worried that she wasn't having the good stuff with them.

She was glad Kolby was teaching her brother to grill. She didn't know how to do it. "Thanks, but I'm really in the zone for writing right now, so once I grab my tuna fish sandwich, I'm heading back to the office to work on the story some more. See you for dinner," she said to Eric.

"Oh, and after lunch, I'm spending the afternoon painting at the library."

"Oh, right." She'd forgotten he'd told her that.

"Yeah, I can't wait. Dottie said I couldn't go over any earlier because of some of the construction work they were doing, so that's why I went to the ranch instead to work. Hal said before he shows up to provide the security watch in the basement, he's having dinner with Tracey and the kids and then he'll be over."

"Okay, I'll see you then."

"Yeah, see you." Eric sounded so happy, she was glad for him.

The other news would have to wait until later. She hoped he wouldn't be upset with her for not telling him sooner. She called Larry Pierce next, since he was the resident lawyer in Yuma Town. Ted's mate, Stella, worked for him as his law clerk and Rosalie wanted advice about this whole business.

Once she talked to Stella, and then Larry, Rosalie learned what she had always known—without Eric's father's consent, she couldn't legally adopt him.

"But," Larry assured her, "we'll do whatever we can to help you keep him here."

She thanked him, hoping he really could do something for them with regard to keeping her brother at home with her, if his dad showed up and wanted to remove him from here.

THAT EVENING, Kolby arrived at the mansion for dinner and gave Rosalie a hug and kiss. Right away, he noticed the Turkish rugs had been removed.

"Stryker and Ricky came by to roll them up and take them away to be cleaned," Rosalie said, the kittens playing chase all over the wooden floor for now.

"Oh, good."

Just then, Eric called Rosalie and told her he was still painting at the library, but Dottie and her mate, Jack, were having him come to dinner and then Jack was bringing him home. "I'll be working on the library for the next couple of days also. I won't be working at the ranch until I get it done."

"Okay, that sounds good. I'll just have dinner with Kolby and let him know that you are not going to work at the ranch until you finish the painting projects at the library. I know you need to get this done." She winked at Kolby. Maybe they could have a moment together before Eric arrived home.

"Hey," Kolby said to her as she ended the call with her brother, "I'm all for holding off on dinner for a little bit if you want to do something else first."

She picked up the kittens, left them in their room, and then grabbed Kolby's hand and headed for the stairs. "For sure."

"Did you tell Eric about the possibility his father is coming to see him?"

"No, not yet. I wanted to speak to him in person instead. The guy who's been breaking into the mansion might not be his father either. I don't want to upset him needlessly when he's enjoying painting."

THAT NIGHT, Hal arrived to serve on guard duty at the same time Jack dropped Eric off. Jack said to Hal, "You know any of us at the CSF can take a shift to watch the mansion at night, if you need us to spell you." Jack worked as one of the special agents with the Cougar Special Forces Division, CSFD, though it was also known as CSF."

"Yeah, Dan talked to Leyton this morning about it already. Just in case we're tied up with sheriff business and some of you are free to serve on guard duty," Hal said.

"Leyton?" Rosalie asked, not remembering who that was.

"He runs the CSF branch here in Yuma Town and he's Deputy Sheriff Stryker's twin brother," Jack said.

Rosalie nodded. "Ah, okay." It would take time for her to learn who was who in Yuma Town.

"I'm beat what with ranching and painting at the library, not to mention getting up so early. I'll be painting on the mural all day tomorrow and then my birthday party is tomorrow night, so I'm going to go to bed," Eric said.

That was a first! "I need to talk to you first," Rosalie said.

"Well, I'll get out of your hair," Jack said. "I need to help put the kids to bed back home."

Eric thanked Jack for bringing him home and everyone said good night to Jack.

Kolby waited for Rosalie to say she wanted him to stay or not when she talked to Eric. She did and took Kolby's hand to lead him into the living room.

"I'm going to head down to the basement," Hal said, then he left them alone.

"What's going on?" Eric asked, taking a seat on one of the sofas, looking too tired to be worried about anything.

Rosalie and Kolby took a seat on the other sofa. She explained what Ava had said to her about the man coming to see Eric. "Nina hadn't had any visions pertaining to the intruder."

"But it could be someone else. Not my dad," Eric said.

"Yeah. I mean, we have no idea who it could be still," Rosalie said.

"But you think he's the most likely suspect," Eric ran his hands through his hair. "Okay."

Rosalie chewed on her bottom lip.

Eric smiled, got up from the sofa, and hugged her. "You know what Mom always said. You borrow trouble. If it is my dad, we'll see what he has to say. If it isn't, then the sheriff can lock him up for breaking and entering."

"Okay." But Eric's words didn't settle Rosalie's anxiety about it.

Kolby ran his hand over Rosalie's back. "Eric's right. With all the getting up to check on things in the middle of the night and making sure Ricky was okay, I'm ready to go back to bed too, if you are," Kolby said to Rosalie.

Rosalie smiled. "That's for sure. I kept meaning to take a nap sometime during the day, but when I'm writing, I just get wrapped up in the story."

Eric went to the cat room and carried the kittens to the stairs, then they all headed up them. Eric was ahead of them, but turned, frowned, and said, "You did remember to get me a birthday cake, didn't you?"

"I sure did. You'll love it, and all the party favors came in. I was going to help you put them together in the canvas sacks, but if you don't have time because you're painting the murals at the library tomorrow, I can do it myself," Rosalie said.

"No, I want to help you. So what kind of a cake did you get?"

"Chocolate, but the rest of it is a surprise."

Eric smiled. "Hmm, good. Chocolate is my favorite. What about ice cream? I love chocolate mint chip and butter pecan but get vanilla too in case someone doesn't like the other flavors."

"We'll make sure we have it," Rosalie said, figuring whoever brought the cake could pick up the ice cream and she'd pay him or her for it.

Then they all wished each other a good night and Eric went up the tower stairs to his bedroom and locked the door.

When Kolby and Rosalie entered her bedroom and shut the door, Kolby said, "Eric took the news that his dad might be showing up to see him well."

"I hope he wasn't trying to be all brave for you," Rosalie said. "He really admires you and I don't want him to hide how he feels. He needs to talk about it."

"Do you want me to talk to him right now?"

She sighed. "Sure. Thanks, Kolby. I really think the notion has hit him harder than he's letting on." Rosalie gave Kolby a hug, so appreciating him for taking on the role of a big brother to Eric.

"No problem. Sometimes a guy just needs another guy to talk to."

13

Wanting to make sure that Eric wasn't upset that the intruder might be his dad, Kolby went up to the tower bedroom and knocked on the door. "Hey, it's me. Listen, if you want to talk about anything—"

The door unlocked and Eric opened it. His eyes were red with tears.

Kolby gave him a hug. "This man might not be your dad."

"I know. And I know that I said that to Rosalie about not borrowing trouble because she always does that. But damn, if it is him—what if he wants me to live with him in Alaska?"

Kolby worried that Eric might not have a choice. "He might not even want that. He might have finally learned your mother and stepfather died and he decided it was time to check on you."

"Nearly sixteen years too late."

"Yeah, I totally agree. We'll work it out somehow."

Eric's eyes rounded. "What if he *makes* me go with him? What if I don't have a choice?"

"You have a whole town of shifters here for you. We have your back."

"Okay." Eric didn't sound reassured that they could protect him.

Truly, if this was Eric's biological dad and he came for him and he brought a force of his own snow leopard shifter friends with him, they might not have any say in it.

"If you don't feel up to painting on the mural tomorrow—" Kolby knew Dottie would understand.

"No way. I promised, and it really would drive me crazy if I was waiting around the house all day to see if the dude showed up."

"All right, but if you change your mind, Dottie will understand."

"No. She's eager to see what the last finished mural looks like. Besides, we have no idea when he's going to show up. It could be anytime, tomorrow, next week, tonight even. I'm not redoing my schedule because of him. I still say it might not even be him. Would he even know my birthday?" Eric scoffed. "He left before I was born. I'm all right, really. I appreciate you talking to me though. I was feeling a little...uhm, down."

"It's to be expected when you hadn't heard from him in all these years. Well, good night. Come see us if you need to."

"Thanks." Then Eric locked his door on Kolby's departure, and Kolby couldn't help but feel bad about Eric and his situation.

Eric had finally found a home here, friends, a place to work, homeschooling activities, people to teach him how to drive, and a whole cat shifter community to be with.

When Kolby returned to Rosalie's room, she was waiting for him to rejoin her, the light on still. "How was he?"

"I'm glad I talked with him. I think he's worried, feeling upset. I think he felt a little better after I talked with him."

She snuggled with Kolby. "He's loving it here so much."

"I know. Truly, we'll do everything in our power to keep him here."

He was so glad she and Eric had moved into the mansion. But he worried that if Eric's father did turn up to take him to Alaska with him, Rosalie would go too. Then what? Kolby didn't want to leave his life behind either, his friends, his family. Especially when he had been taking care of his own brother for years, so he knew what that was like.

Losing Rosalie wasn't an option either. Hell, here he was worried about how Eric was feeling—though he was just a kid and he had fewer options to him—but now Kolby was just as anxious about everything.

"Go to sleep," Rosalie said, running her hand over his furrowed brow. "Everything will work out eventually."

Only if Rosalie and Eric stayed here. Anything else would be a total nightmare.

EARLY THE NEXT MORNING, everyone was awake. Rosalie hadn't gotten enough sleep and Kolby had tossed and turned all night too. She had worried about the situation with Eric and how he was feeling. She felt she had two options—if the stranger was Eric's father and he wanted to take him to Alaska—she could go with them and write her books up there, giving up her newfound friends here, but most of all, Kolby, whom she really loved. She couldn't expect him to leave his family and friends to join her in Alaska either. Or she could stay here and feel as though she had abandoned her brother to a virtual stranger. His biological father, sure, but one he didn't know at all.

She hurried to get dressed, ready for Mrs. Fitz to bring them pastries, and send Jack and Eric on their way to the library, and Kolby to the ranch. Then she had to decorate for the birthday party. She planned to work on transforming the mansion and greenhouse into a Halloween party place after Eric's birthday party tonight. Worrying about what might not be—was a waste of time.

Kolby made Eric special chocolate waffles topped with whipped cream, chocolate chips, and strawberries this morning when Mrs. Fitz arrived with the pastries. Rosalie had forgotten to tell Kolby that Mrs. Fitz was bringing them treats!

"Would you like to come in and join us?" Rosalie asked Mrs. Fitz.

"Thanks, but I have to get back to the shop. On another subject, I've got some friends in high places who are searching for Eric's father to learn what we can about him. It always helps to know what we're up against."

Kolby joined Rosalie at the front door. "Mrs. Fitz is retired CIA."

"Oh, wow, how exciting." Maybe Mrs. Fitz could get somewhere with some inquiries, Rosalie was thinking.

"It was. I still have friends there, and well, just in case we need any ammunition, so to speak, we'll learn whatever we can about him."

Rosalie gave her a hug, startling Mrs. Fitz, but she smiled and hugged her back.

"We're all in this together," Mrs. Fitz said.

"Thank you. We so appreciate it. And thanks for the great pastries."

"You're welcome. We'll talk later."

Then Rosalie felt a little more lighthearted and she and Kolby returned to the dining room with the pastries.

"Mate the guy already," Eric said to Rosalie, surprising her. "Hey, anyone who can make this kind of a breakfast when we're all half asleep is worth hanging on to."

She laughed. "Do you want to be my forever mate?" she asked Kolby.

His face brightened in a sunshiny smile. "Hell, yeah. I thought you'd never ask."

She laughed again, figuring he was just playing along.

"The news will be out this morning that we have another mated cougar couple in Yuma Town," Hal said, then took another bite of his chocolate waffle.

Even though Kolby had made the waffles special for Eric's birthday treat, everyone had wanted them too. But as an extra treat, they enjoyed Mrs. Fitz's pastries also. When they were finished eating, Rosalie said, "You guys go. Get to work. I've got the dishes."

Kolby glanced at Rosalie, still smiling, waiting for her to confirm she had meant it. She just smiled, her cheeks heating a bit.

"Hell, are you serious?" Kolby asked Rosalie.

"Unless you don't want to." She figured that they needed to decide on this one way or another. It didn't mean it would be any easier to make a decision concerning what to do about the situation with Eric, should his father want to take him to Alaska, but she wanted Kolby to be her mate in any case.

They could wait months, years, but she knew it wasn't going to change the way she felt about him. She couldn't have met a kinder, more generous cougar than him. Not to mention he was hot, cooked delicious meals, was a great helper, and a wonderful lover!

"No way am I waiting to be asked twice. I had planned on asking you after Eric's birthday party."

"Do you want to wait?"

He laughed. "No way!"

Hal slapped Kolby on the back. "Wait until all the cubs arrive."

"You gotta give Kolby the day off because it could be a life-or-death matter otherwise," Eric said. "You know, because he'll be so busy thinking about getting back to my sister tonight that he won't be doing his job right at the ranch."

Everyone laughed. Rosalie couldn't believe her brother would tell Kolby's boss to give Kolby time off to mate her.

"You can have the rest of the week off. You still have this business going on with the intruder, who might be Eric's father, and I suspect Rosalie wants to start getting the mansion ready for the Halloween party. We'll all help with it, but you can help her with some of it this week when you're not busy with other—important stuff," Hal said.

Kolby smiled at Rosalie and pulled her in for a hug. "Thanks, Boss."

"Think nothing of it. If I didn't give you the time off, Tracey wouldn't let me hear the end of it. And Ted? Same thing."

"Thanks," Kolby said again.

"Okay, well, you'd better hop to it before Eric's home again. We'll talk again soon," Hal said.

Eric gave Kolby a hug on the way out the door. "Welcome to the family." She hugged Eric goodbye, wishing him a happy birthday.

Then Hal and Eric headed out to his truck. Rosalie and Kolby waved goodbye and when they drove off, Kolby shouted, "Yes!"

Rosalie smiled, and then she and Kolby returned to the dining room where she picked up the kittens that were chasing each other all over, and they took them to their cat room. Then Rosalie grabbed Kolby's hand—forget about doing the dishes right this minute—and led him up the stairs to her bedroom. *Their* bedroom. She realized he would be part owner of the mansion also. They needed to get married. They needed to go on a honeymoon too. She'd want Eric to stay with someone during that time. Now that he had several new friends, she was sure someone would take him in. Even Hal or Ted would probably do it. Heck, he could stay in the bunkhouse with the other ranch hands. He'd probably get a kick out of it.

Then Rosalie and Kolby were stripping each other out of their clothes, carelessly tossing them onto the floor. The two of them landed on the mattress, all arms and legs and hot bodies, ready for this. He was on top of her, his legs between hers, feeling so ready for her, his strong hands caressing her shoulders, his gaze wickedly seductive. But then she rolled, and he was beneath her, and she was on top of him, her legs cradling his now. Both were smiling when she grabbed his hands, pinned them to the mattress, and leaned down to kiss his mouth. He was so tantalizingly hers, and she couldn't be more grateful for that.

Already her heart and his were pounding wildly. No one had ever made her feel like this—so lustful, so desperate, her pheromones triggering his. He rolled her onto her back. Then he was pressing his rigid erection against her mound, leaning against her, kissing her breasts. His mouth felt heavenly on her breasts, his tongue lathing her rigid, sensitive nipple, his lips closing onto it and sucking. His free hand massaged her other breast. Ohmigod, her mate was her perfect lover.

Her body pulsed with craving as she gazed up into his eyes. He smiled down at her with a look of lustful desire and a hint of a smile. A little dimple appeared. She loved his dimples—they made him look sexy and so loveable.

"You are so soft and warm and sweet," he said, then licked the other nipple, sucked on it, sending a thrill straight to her belly and lower.

"You're a dream come true." She knew she was dreaming that she was truly with him, and he was hers.

"So are you." He pressed kisses all the way up her collarbone, to her throat, and then to her lips and she savored his kisses.

Her tongue slipped between his parted lips and tasted him, teased his tongue, stroked, and appeased him. He kissed her slowly back, lingering, stealing her thoughts. While she was enjoying him, he slid his hand between her parted legs and began to stroke her nubbin. Oh, ecstatic joy. She savored his touch, his musky scent, the feeling of his hot fingers stroking her into a state of bliss.

She bit his lip gently, so caught up in the whole wonderful experience. She was suddenly coming with breathless anticipation. Then she was over the top and crashing to earth just as he was pushing into her with his engorged erection. She was blazing hot as he began to thrust into her, sweeping her into the next phase of their seduction.

KOLBY DROVE his heavy erection deep inside of Rosalie's silky, wet sheath, pulling halfway out and thrusting again. She was so snug around him, gripping him like a vice. He slipped his hands under her buttocks and pulled her hard against him. She bent her knees, deepening his penetration. She felt damn good around him as he was rocking into her, and she was meeting his thrusts with enthusiasm.

He drove into her faster and harder, his mouth capturing hers. She was his for now and forever. She was just the person he'd needed in his life when he really had thought he was perfectly happy with the way things were. But being in the throes of passion with his mate like this was nothing short of a miracle. He was thrusting hard when he felt her tensing, and he knew she was going to come again. He kissed her mouth, tonguing her, and then she cried out and he erupted inside her, collapsing on her and just holding her in his arms. He was glad

Hal had given him the time off to be with Rosalie like this. Making love to her once was never enough.

"I love you, you sexy, big cat," Rosalie said, then kissed him again.

He rolled over and pulled her onto his stomach. "I knew you were the only one for me. I love you right back, honey."

AFTER KOLBY and Rosalie woke much later from their glorious nap, they took a shower and dressed. Kolby said, "We probably should have talked about this before, but as a contingency plan, if the intruder was Eric's dad and he comes to take him to Alaska, I will go anywhere or do anything for you and Eric. So if it means moving to Alaska to be near him, we can do it. That's if we can't convince Eric's dad to leave him here. I mean, his dad could even stay here if he likes. Not that he would stay at the mansion, but that he could live in Yuma Town and get to know Eric that way."

"Oh, I hadn't thought of that. But thanks for offering to move. I just don't know what to think. Of course, we'll just have to wait and see what happens." Then she smiled. "Would you like to help me decorate for Eric's birthday?"

"I can't think of anything more fun to do."

"Uhm, I'm sure the kids will want to see the greenhouse while they are at Eric's birthday party. Since we plan to make it the haunted house for Halloween, do you want to help me clean up the glass all over the ground inside there, just to make sure it's safe enough to walk through?"

"Yeah. Let's do it," Kolby said.

They both got some garden gloves and a couple of trash containers.

"We can save the glass shards. Dr. Kate loves to work with

glass to create stained glass art. Since this glass is so old, she'll love to have it," Kolby said.

"Wonderful. I always love it when things can be recycled."

With the two of them working on it, it didn't take them long to finish up that work. "Do we leave the partially broken windows for the effect at Halloween, or would it be safer to remove the broken windows and replace them, or even leave them empty until after the party?" she asked.

"I think we should remove the windows and replace them. We can add cobwebs to them, but for safety reasons, we should make sure it's safe and weatherproof, so installing windows would be a good idea. I can call someone and have them measure and order the glass."

For a hundred reasons and more, Kolby was just the right mate for her.

AFTER PAINTING all day at the library, Eric rode home with Jack for his birthday party. "I'm staying the night as your security detail," Jack said to Rosalie, "since Eric is returning to the library to finish painting the second mural in the morning. I can just take him with me when I'm finished with my detail."

"Jack said he'd let me drive to the library too," Eric said, sounding elated. He was helping Rosalie to fill the gift bags for his friends.

"Oh, that's great," Rosalie said, smiling. "What about eating dinner?"

"Oh, Eric invited me to have hot dogs at the bonfire," Jack said. "I couldn't pass the opportunity up."

"You too, sis," Eric said. "And Kolby too. I didn't think I had to invite you, that you'd just be there. Besides, if the intruder shows up, we need to be a unified force."

"Sure, I love roasted hot dogs," Rosalie said.

Kolby smiled. "Well, since Rosalie and I are mated, I'm your big brother, and of course, I have to have hot dogs and s'mores and the rest at the bonfire for your birthday party."

Eric whooped. Jack congratulated them for being mated cougars. "Oh, and I nearly forgot." Jack went outside to his truck and came back inside with a gift basket of honey and honeycomb candles, olive oil with lavender essential oils, and packages of chocolate-covered bridge mix, butter pecans, salted cashews, cranberry nut blend, cherry almonds, and honey sea salt peanuts. "This is from all of us at the CSF and our families."

"Oh, how wonderful," Rosalie said, Eric reaching in to check out the packages of nuts and agreeing with her.

And now Kolby would be the recipient also.

AFTER ERIC GOT HOME from finishing the mural at the library about one, he hadn't been able to sit still. He'd helped Rosalie decorate with balloons, streamers and Kolby had worked with Eric to set up the bonfire. He'd spent time playing with the kittens, but he was anxious for the party to begin.

Kolby and Jasper had headed into town to pick up the new windows for the greenhouse because they'd just gotten them in. When everyone was supposed to arrive at the party, no one did.

"They'll be here," Rosalie said.

"Kolby and Jasper aren't even here," Eric said.

"They will be. You know Kolby said he and Jasper might be a little late in arriving because of picking up the windows for the greenhouse."

Eric glanced at the wall clock again. "Everyone's twenty minutes late."

She knew he was upset, trying not to show that he was. But

she knew there had to be a simple explanation for why everyone was late in arriving.

Finally, Bobby texted Eric and Rosalie waited to hear what was going on.

Eric let out a big relief of breath. "They're coming."

Rosalie smiled. "I knew they would be."

"There was a big accident on the road coming out here. No one was hurt, but an eighteen-wheeler jackknifed and they're still clearing off the road so that the cars can get through."

"Oh, how awful, but I'm glad everyone's okay."

"Yeah, me too." Eric smiled. "You were right. Everyone's coming."

Sure enough, within the half hour, cars were arriving. Some of the kids had carpooled, and then they all piled out to start the celebration. Amy, Bobby's mom, had brought the cake and the ice cream. Both Eric and Rosalie loved the cake.

All of the kids thought it was cool and the boys wanted one like it for their birthdays. Then all the kids wanted to see the mansion next.

Eric eagerly showed them the rooms all over the mansion, but he first showed off the kittens.

"Ooh, yeah, you got my favorites," Avery said, Andy agreeing.

Eric told them their names and then everyone wanted to pet them before he put them in the cat room. They all loved it.

"You've got to do a cat mural for Great Aunt Mae," Avery said. "She would love it."

"Yeah, that would be so cool," Andy said. "We'll talk to her about it."

Eric smiled.

But then everyone wanted to see the basement and the greenhouse too.

"Wow, this is where the mystery person keeps coming," one of the kids said from down in the basement.

Rosalie smiled. Then the kids all raced outside to see the greenhouse. She heard Kolby pull up in his Jeep and Jasper drove up in a pickup and parked.

She went out to meet them and gave Kolby a hug. "Eric was upset everyone arrived late."

"I heard about the accident on the road. It was cleared before we reached the area. But I got all the windows. Thankfully, I had Jasper to help me."

"Eric and the others are at the greenhouse if you want to join them," Rosalie told Jasper.

"Yeah, thanks. Are you going to tell Rosalie about the gift?" Then Jasper left to catch up with the kids.

"Yeah, I want to give my Jeep to Eric so he can learn to drive it. I've had it repainted and tuned up, if that's okay with you," Kolby said.

"Oh, yeah, that would be great. I didn't know what I would do about a vehicle, and I'm sure he'll be thrilled."

"Okay, great. I figure I'll give him the keys to the Jeep tomorrow morning, before he returns to the library to finish the mural," Kolby said.

"That will be wonderful. Should we run as big cougars separately from the teens tonight?" Rosalie asked.

"Yeah, we'll let the teens have their fun. Jasper, being the eldest of the teens, can watch out for them."

"They're going to run early, I bet, after the bonfire, just so they can see Eric in his snow leopard coat again."

"I'm sure you're right."

Then they went inside, and she fixed them some hot cocoa.

"I can't believe we haven't had any more visitations from the unknown person who was in the basement," Kolby said.

"I can. What with Dan's deputy sheriffs and now the CSF

agents taking a night each day and the security cameras, whoever it was is staying clear of the mansion. When the law enforcement officers end their stay here, then what? I don't want you staying down in the basement. Or I'd have to stay down there with you," Rosalie said.

"To protect me?" He cocked a brow.

"No, I need you in my bed at night for all that loving."

He smiled, but when the teens ended up back in the house, they switched to another topic.

"And here is my art studio," Eric said.

"No way. Too cool, dude," Andy said.

"Hey, we heard your sister has magic at her fingertips. Will she show it to us?" Avery asked.

Rosalie showed them what she could do—from creating a ball of light to teleporting books and birthday presents all over the room.

"Can you see ghosts?" Andy asked.

"No. But I hear Chase, Stryker, and Leyton can."

Andy glanced at Eric. He nodded. Andy turned back to Rosalie. "You have a gardener in your greenhouse."

Rosalie's jaw dropped. "A ghost."

"Yeah. She's nice. But if you feel unusual cold spots once the windows have all been replaced in there, that's probably her."

Kolby rubbed Rosalie's back, but then she gathered her composure. "What about the house? The basement?"

"No. Not that I saw."

She let out her breath in relief.

Andy smiled. "Eric put me in charge of ghost stories for tonight at the bonfire while we're eating our hot dogs and other stuff, since I have real ghost stories to tell."

"Oh, that's wonderful," Rosalie said.

Then they all went outside to enjoy roasting hot dogs, s'mores, and began pigging out on chips and drinking sodas.

The night air was chilly, but the bonfire kept them warm, and they were glad there wasn't any rain tonight.

After Andy ate his fill, he began telling ghost stories, the firelight casting an eerie glow over the partygoers.

"So one time on a stormy night I was helping my mom remove wallpaper from my sister's and my bathroom. Uhm, we had sort of splattered toothpaste on it when we were brushing our teeth. Don't ask how. But the bleach in the toothpaste took the color out of the wallpaper and it was peeling in places. Mom wanted us to remove the wallpaper and that's what we were doing," Andy said.

"On a stormy night," Eric said, smiling.

"Yeah, lightning, thunder, lots of heavy rain, pitch black out, scary."

"When you make a big change to rooms, spirits can be disturbed, I've heard," Jasper said.

Rosalie was thinking about all the changes they were making to the property!

"I heard this delightful music playing and I asked my mom and my sister what it was that they were playing. And then it stopped. We went to look for the sound of the tunes, but I was the only one who had heard them. Our neighbors were musicians who made music, but I'd never heard them playing at their home and there was no music playing anywhere else," Andy said. "I even thought maybe it was a passing car with their music on high, but that would have been way across cornfields."

"Your mother and sister didn't hear the music playing before it stopped?" Rosalie asked.

"No. But they helped me look for it. They believed me."

Everyone was quiet.

"I hear things that others don't. Sometimes I see things that others don't. Like the gardener in the greenhouse. She was watering the plants by hand, talking to them, loving them."

"What about when we have the haunted house in there?" Eric asked. "Do you think it will upset her?"

That's what Rosalie was afraid of.

"I can tell her what we're going to do," Andy said.

"You can talk to them?" Eric asked, sounding shocked.

"Uh, yeah. Sometimes it helps when someone who can see them, can talk to them."

"Oh, well, yeah, thanks, we need you to do that," Eric said.

Rosalie was surprised Eric didn't appear to be upset about the notion they had a ghost in the greenhouse. But then she figured he wasn't going to be doing any gardening, while she would love to.

"Did the gardener tell you her story?" Bobby asked Andy.

"I didn't ask. Maybe when Chase does the séance for Halloween, we can learn who she is and all about her," Andy said.

"Tell them about the rabbit that hopped into your bed," Andy's twin sister said.

"Well, we didn't have a rabbit, but a previous owner did, and their pet had died of old age. So one night I was sound asleep and suddenly I felt the rabbit jump into the bed. It scared me half to death. You have to know the ghosts seem real to me. My first thought was that it was there for real. That Avery had somehow talked mom into allowing her to have a rabbit that I didn't know about. When I went to her room, carrying the rabbit with me, Avery couldn't see the rabbit at all."

Avery laughed. "Yeah, he said he had my rabbit and woke me up over it. He even woke Mom up to ask her, not believing me. Then we realized he was having one of his ghostly encounters."

"Did you take the rabbit back to bed with you?" Eric asked.

"Nah. He vanished. But he comes to join me at night most nights and sleeps with me. Luckily, he doesn't scare me any longer."

"Wow," Bobby said. "I don't think I could ever get used to that."

"Me either," Eric said. "I have a hard enough time with the intruder in the basement."

"But he's or she's real," Rosalie said.

"That's worse than a ghost," Sissy said.

Once they were done with ghost stories, they went inside to open presents and have cake and ice cream. They gave Eric his birthday presents—art supplies, video games, art books, and a Yuma Town T-shirt featuring a snow leopard. He got a kick out of that. Rosalie gave Eric cowboy boots, chaps, a couple of western shirts, and a Stetson so he'd be ready to be a cowboy. Eric was so glad he would really fit in at the ranch now wearing his own brand-new clothes.

"Hey, dude, we're going running as big cats," Jasper said, "right?"

"Yeah, let's do this," Eric said, sounding eager to show off his snow leopard coat.

Rosalie could tell this had been the best party Eric had ever had.

The girls went into one of the meeting rooms to change and shift and the guys used another.

Jack was staying in the basement just in case the intruder showed up, so no big cat run for him.

Rosalie and Kolby took off on their own to enjoy their big cat run while the kids all headed in a different direction. Kolby planned to take some of the kids home after the party since they didn't know when it would really end. Jasper promised to take the rest home before he returned to the ranch.

Rosalie licked Kolby's muzzle. She was so ready for the party to end so they could retire to bed. She'd never wanted to be in bed as much as she did now that she had Kolby in her life.

14

T hat night at the party, Kolby had expected for the intruder to show up because it had been Eric's birthday, but he didn't. Maybe with all the people there, he decided not to. Or maybe he wasn't Eric's father, or if he was, maybe he didn't know his birth date. In any case, Jack stayed overnight, but they didn't have any disturbances.

At breakfast, Eric said to Rosalie, "You know what this means, don't you?"

"What *what* means?" she asked, genuinely perplexed. She glanced at Kolby.

"You know I have my learner's permit to drive already. Now I'm sixteen. Once I take my driver's test, I can drive without an adult having to ride with me." Eric smiled broadly. "You can continue to teach me to drive, Kolby."

"Actually," Kolby said, "that's part of the ranch hands and my birthday gift to you. Even Ted said he'd come and help you learn how to drive."

"Oh, wow," Eric said, looking just thrilled.

Kolby had offered to teach Eric to drive before, but she

hadn't expected all the guys to teach him. She loved being here because everyone was so willing to help with so much. "If you still need me to help you practice, I'll certainly do that."

"Good. Because if I'm going to work at the ranch, I need to drive myself," Eric said.

"We were talking about that too," Kolby said. "We're going to put in a cattle guard and open up the fence in one spot between our property. Hal's already putting in a road so that none of us will have to drive the long away around on the main road to get from the mansion to the ranch, if that's all right with you."

"It would be perfect. Then Eric could even just drive to the ranch by himself before he has his driver's license, if he's not driving on the main road—*after* he gets a number of lessons under his belt," Rosalie said.

"And we can have a walking path for when we want to cross as big cats," Kolby said.

"That'll be wonderful." She loved the idea because they had a lot more acreage than she and Eric and Kolby had so if they wanted to run on Hal and Tracey's property, they could easily do that. Sure, they could jump the fence, which is what Eric must have done when Kolby first saw him in his snow leopard coat, but she was thinking about making it easier for everyone that way.

Kolby handed the Jeep keys to Eric. "This is my birthday present to you. No driving it by yourself until we say so and that means having several lessons first."

"Your Jeep? I can have your Jeep? For real? Not just to learn on? No way." Eric couldn't have looked any more thrilled than he did now.

"Yeah. She's all yours. Take good care of her."

"Yeah, I will." Eric gave him a hug. "So when can we have some more lessons? Rosalie let me drive a little, but I think I made her too nervous."

Kolby laughed. "Rosalie can give them to you during the day, if she's free. When you go in with me to the ranch, I can let you drive and when I'm off, I can take you out to drive."

"Yes!"

Rosalie was so glad everyone was eager to help her brother learn to drive.

FOR THE NEXT TEN DAYS, the sheriff, deputy sheriffs, and special agents with the CSF came to stay at the mansion, waiting for the intruder who never came. Kolby and some of the men had installed the new windows of the greenhouse but no one who was a ghost sensitive had felt any presence while out there at the time. Rosalie was glad.

Kolby had taken her out to the movies twice, a steakhouse restaurant, and a pizza parlor in Loveland—though on the pizza date, they had to take Eric. He promised he'd sit at another table so they could have their intimate date, but they enjoyed being there with him, watching the pizza chefs tossing the dough in the form of pizzas into the air, and having homemade root beer. They'd enjoyed trips on dates to Joe's Mexican Restaurant in Yuma Town and Mrs. Fitz's bakery also for soups and sand-wiches. It didn't matter that Rosalie and Kolby were already mated, planning their wedding for March, but these were their special date nights. They'd also been to the Watering Hole Bar and Grill for dinner one night, and the Cup and Cone as an afternoon Saturday treat.

Eric had even done several extra-curricular activities with other homeschoolers from sewing to woodworking. He had also finished the murals in the Haverton's kids' rooms. They loved them. He was still planning the painting for the Town Hall, and Mrs. Fitz had commissioned a painting from him for her shop even, so he was working on that next. Avery and Andy had spoken to their Great Aunt Mae and she wanted a cat mural done in one of the rooms where she kept her cats. Even Bobby's mom ordered a picture for Bobby for Christmas.

Everyone had also gone to the grand opening of the library where Rosalie and Eric had cut the ribbon at the ceremony, dedicating the library in name to Charity Squire. Rosalie had been so proud of Eric's beautiful murals too. He was so eager to show her the shelf where her whole spell caster series were lined up. She laughed and was thrilled to see them in the new library.

Eric had told her both he and Kolby had made sure Dottie had ordered the books for the library. She thought the world of them for doing it.

After Eric drove Kolby to work at the ranch that morning, Rosalie headed to Yuma Town to pick up groceries and stopped in to talk to Ava about desserts for the Halloween party.

"Oh," Ava said, "Mrs. Fitz and I are making all the desserts. You don't have to worry about it."

"Okay." Rosalie smiled. "That sounds good."

"Everyone wants to share in the decorating and preparing foods. You are just providing the facilities, so you don't have to do anything really."

"Oh, I'll help with the decorations." Rosalie was so excited about it now that she was finished with her brother's birthday party and had turned in her book to her publisher.

Ava's sister, Nina, came into the shop, smiling broadly. On duty, she was wearing her deputy sheriff's uniform and gave her sister a hug. "Well?" Ava asked.

"Yep. We're pregnant too."

Surprised and thrilled to hear the good news, Rosalie smiled at them. "Congratulations, Nina and Ava."

"Thank you!" Ava said. "My mate is thrilled."

"Mine too," Nina said.

Rosalie was thinking she would love to have babies with Kolby. Then she said goodbye to the ladies and headed to the grocery store. Eric called her and she wondered what was up.

"Hey, sis." Then he proceeded to tell her all the things he'd forgotten to add to her grocery list this morning.

She laughed. He always did that to her when he didn't go grocery shopping with her.

"I got it." Then she picked up all the groceries and returned home, put them away, and began bringing out their Halloween decorations. They didn't have enough to really fill the mansion it was so big so she planned to put all the decorations just in the living room. She was glad others would bring decorations that would help to make it look great for the party.

The ranch hands had already said they'd decorate the green-house to turn it into a haunted house. Kolby would take charge of the efforts. Eric was thrilled to help with it.

Dan and the deputy sheriffs were in charge of the haystack maze. Ted and Stella were working on all the scarecrows. Ava and Mrs. Fitz were planning all the desserts. Addie, Dottie, Shannon, and Bridget were in charge of planning the food. The CSF agents Travis, Leyton, and Chet were in charge of the band and stringing orange lights around the manor and greenhouse. Drs. Kate, William, and Vanessa would provide a medical station manned by them, nurses, and vet techs in shifts, just in case anyone was injured during the frivolity.

Stryker, Chase, and Leyton planned to do a séance in the greenhouse. They were setting up battery-operated candles in all of the mansion's windows.

Rosalie would put on a magic show. Nina and Ava wanted to have a fortunetelling "booth." Ava said giving readings used to bother her, but she had grown more used to doing them so they would take turns. Bridget said if anyone wanted her to read their minds, she would.

Rosalie figured Kolby and Eric and she could celebrate her birthday the day after Halloween since they were going to be so busy with the Halloween party.

THE DAY of the Halloween party, the final touches were being made. Rosalie, Kolby, and Eric carved their jack-o'-lanterns and set them in the entryway of the front door. Rosalie had created a witch, Kolby the profile of a horse's head, and Eric outshined them with a beautiful dragon. Then she lit the pumpkins with her special ability.

The party would start at two so that everyone could participate in the hay maze, taking rides on an old wagon through the pumpkin patch filled with scarecrows, and play games while it was light out.

Eric was running back and forth, helping everywhere he could. He was already talking about the feast everyone wanted to have in their big dining room! This was becoming to be known as the party place because of the seating arrangements in the two big dining rooms.

Chase had even worked with a bunch of the teens on the flooring as an extra homeschooling curriculum. They had a blast working on all the stairs' banisters and polishing the floors.

Rosalie, Kolby, and Eric had replaced the counters with granite ones, added a kitchen island with five bar stools, and replaced the sinks with stainless steel. All the rugs had been cleaned. And they'd even bought another widescreen TV, this one to add in the den so that if they wanted to watch different shows, they could. Everything looked just right for the party.

Mrs. Fitz had gotten back with Rosalie about Eric's dad and said, "My sources say he's in the backcountry in Alaska."

"So he wasn't here breaking into the mansion's basement?" Rosalie asked.

"He could have been. It's been weeks since you had an occurrence."

"But Ava said he would come to see Eric," Rosalie said.

"Someone. Not the dad, for sure," Mrs. Fitz reminded her.

"Okay, you're right. Thanks, Mrs. Fitz."

"You're welcome. We're still looking for him, so if he turns up on our radar, we'll let you know."

THAT AFTERNOON, everyone started arriving at the mansion dressed in their costumes: witches, warlocks, Ninja turtle kids, Ariel mermaids, Snow White, Baby Sharks, and pirates. Ava and Nina were wearing fortune telling costumes and were taking turns giving fortunes in one of the meeting rooms. Ava, Mrs. Fitz, Chase's wife, Shannon, and Dottie had taken over the kitchen and dining room to decorate and coordinate food displays.

Because of all the people coming in and out, the kittens were put in the cat room where everyone could come and play with them, but they wouldn't get lost, or be underfoot.

Several people had already asked if Rosalie would mind having the annual Christmas party here, and she agreed. New Year's too, and they were talking about a disco party for that. Too much fun.

But at the Halloween party, Kolby was a wise wizard. Eric was dressed as an elf magic user. Most of the women were sexy sorceresses, including Bridget who was reading Dan's mind, despite him telling her she wouldn't be able to. Mrs. Fitz was Maleficent and she looked magnificent.

The ranch hands were all manning the greenhouse and so they were wearing zombie, mummy, and vampire costumes. Everyone was already having a blast. Chase, Stryker, and Hal had been busy taking the kids through the hay maze earlier on. Ted had been giving hay wagon rides.

Rosalie was teleporting drinks from the kitchen to the dining room tables and had easily drawn a crowd.

"Can you teleport me?" one boy asked.

"Nothing too heavy," Rosalie said. "Maybe up to about twenty pounds. Beyond that, I can't lift anything for long with my mental powers. So if your dad runs the car into a ditch, I couldn't move it. But"—she pointed at Travis's phone in his hand—"I can make electronic devices go off."

Travis's phone rang and he nearly dropped it. He looked at the Caller ID. "It's blank." He tried answering it, but there was no one there.

"Now that is the coolest thing," Kolby said.

She showed off her ability to produce a light in her hands, and then she was exhausted from the mental workout. She smiled. "Okay, onto the next great adventure."

Everyone there clapped.

Rosalie felt since it was her and Eric and Kolby's place, she had to actually host the event, but Kolby took her hand and led her outside, not about to allow her to miss out on enjoying the party. She so appreciated him.

She had been forbidden from going through the maze while they were setting up things so that it would be a surprise for her. The same with the haunted greenhouse. After she had seen the replacement of all the broken windows, she hadn't been allowed in there while they were turning it into a haunted house. She hoped the spirit living there wouldn't be upset by all the wild goings ons.

Thankfully, everyone knew everyone, so if the intruder showed up, they'd know he didn't belong, so he wouldn't be able to crash the party without them realizing it.

"The maze is made like a triangle?" Rosalie asked Kolby as he led her to it.

"A witch's hat," Kolby said, leaning over to kiss Rosalie before they entered the maze.

Green beads covered the entrance, and they pushed through the beads to start walking through the maze. Eerie green lights colored the stacks of hay as they made their way hand in hand through the beginning of the maze.

A witch cackled up from the top of the bales of hay, startling Rosalie and she screamed. Then laughed. It was Bridget, a Hocus Pocus witch.

"I can read your mind," Bridget said.

"I bet. You scared me to pieces." Rosalie laughed again. "That's what you read."

"Yep. Have fun you two." Then Bridget disappeared on the other side of the haystacks and Rosalie was wondering if she'd heard them and wanted to scare them or was lost and wanted to sneak a peek over the wall to see if that was the exit.

They hadn't gotten very far before they ran into a warlock, this one Travis, Bridget's mate, also a special agent with CSF. "I cast a spell over you," Travis said.

Rosalie cast her spell of light and Travis smiled. "I haven't quite mastered that spell yet, but your ability is damn cool," Travis said.

Rosalie smiled. "I'm so glad others here have abilities so I don't feel like the odd man out."

"No way, but I certainly am."

Kolby shook his head. "Me too."

"Oh, Kolby, you have all kinds of special abilities." Rosalie smiled at him.

Travis chuckled. "I'm not touching that with a ten-foot pole, as they say."

Then she and Kolby continued on their way. This was so great. At one dead end, they found light sticks with a sign that said: *Take one.*

They grabbed one and then continued on their way, lighting it. It cast an eerie pink light, mixing with the green ones from up above. They had started off in another direction and suddenly ran into three Hocus Pocus witches—Shannon, Tracey, and Bridget. The ladies were running through the maze in their adorable costumes.

"Hocus pocus," Shannon said, waving her hands in the air as if she were going to cast a spell.

But Rosalie cast her light spell and tossed it at a stack of hay the ladies were standing next to and they all screamed.

"She has powerful magic," Tracey said. "Let's begone."

Bridget laughed and agreed, and the three vanished down another path, their long colorful skirts, purple, blue, and green fabrics swishing as they hurried off, still laughing. They were so cute, and this was already the best Halloween ever!

Kolby and Rosalie headed down a different path and they ran into Chase, dressed in a midnight blue cloak and gown. He stomped his wizardly staff on the dirt path and frowned at them. "Have you seen three witches come through here?" He scowled, looking perfectly lethal and Rosalie smiled.

"They went that way." Rosalie totally misdirected him.

"Aye, thanks."

Kolby laughed. When Chase was gone, Kolby said, "You know the next time you're driving a little over the speed limit and Chase is patrolling the area, he could ticket you, for steering him wrong."

She laughed. "He better not. My wizardry skills are much more powerful than his."

"I'll say." Kolby kissed her cheek, and they came to another dead end.

"Are you sure there's a way out of this?" she asked.

"Yeah, we have to reach the tip of the witch's hat."

"Okay. I figured we were headed that way but—"

"The tip of the hat is bent and curled."

"Ah, okay." Then they found a little table with scented candles on it. *Please Take One*, said the sign. She smelled several of the candles and decided on the cinnamon one for Christmas. She handed it to Kolby to carry.

He smiled at her. He was already carrying their light stick also and his wizard's staff.

Then they continued on their way, finding Ricky in his steampunk wizard costume, since he wanted to be a wizard like so many of the other men, but he loved steampunk. "Have you seen Mandy?"

"Not yet," Rosalie said, and then Ricky shook his head.

"Those witches of Eastwick have led my lovely mate astray," Ricky said.

They laughed. Rosalie and Kolby continued down one maze path and then another, dead end after dead end.

"Don't you remember how to get through here?" she teased Kolby.

"I sure do." He smiled down at her and then they met up with three wizards—Dan dressed in all blue, Hal wearing green emerald, and Leyton dressed in silver. They all looked great.

They inclined their heads in greeting, Dan saying, "You wouldn't happen to know the way out of here, would you?"

"Nay," Kolby said, motioning with his own wizard's staff to the sky, "or we would be out of here by now."

Rosalie smiled. "He won't tell me the way out either."

Dan smiled. "Aye, a wizard who cannot keep his secrets is not worthy of being one of us."

Then the three of them passed Kolby and Rosalie. "I'm so glad everyone dressed up for this," she said. "This is so much fun."

"We all love costume time for Halloween or for other fun occasions. I don't think there's anyone in town who doesn't like to participate."

"That's wonderful."

Before they made it very far, they saw Dr. Kate, her nurse, Mandy, and their veterinarian, Vanessa, dressed as the *Witches of Eastwick*.

"Ladies," Kolby said, giving them a wide birth.

They smiled at him, waving their wands and passing them by.

"I love their long gowns," Rosalie said.

"I love your sexy short dress," he said.

"Oh, thanks. Do you think we should have told them Ricky was looking for Mandy?" She paused.

"Nope. After all the twists and turns in the maze that we made, I have no idea where Ricky could be, and knowing him, Ricky's just playing a role. If he really wanted to find Mandy, he'd ring her up."

"Okay. We'd better not get in trouble with your brother if that's not the case." Rosalie charged ahead again. "I think I sense the opening this way." She pulled Kolby down the path and came to a dead end. She laughed and he laughed too. "I guess I don't have any spidery senses to help with finding my way out of mazes."

They turned around and she led him down three more different paths, but then she was certain this one was the one that exited from the maze. She raced to the end and sure enough, they were outside, and she hugged Kolby. "That was great!"

"Do you want to eat now?"

"I want to go to the haunted greenhouse first. I'm dying to see how it was decorated."

"Okay, if you're ready to get scared..."

She smiled. "I am." How scary could it really be?

15

K olby opened the creaking door to the greenhouse, and they heard rats squeaking. They were probably from a soundtrack, but the squealing sounded like it was coming from real rats. Hot air blew over their heads, and then cold. She shivered and Kolby rubbed her arm. A glowing, blue neon skeleton hovered near the entrance. Two skulls sat next to bubbling potions lit up with neon green lights. Several leathery bats were suspended from the ceiling, swaying as if in flight. Old books were stacked on one of the garden tables next to a bunch of colorful, bubbling, potions bottles lit up with neon rainbow lights. Someone's arching, black Halloween cat was near the potions, its yellow-green eyes glowing as it stared at them, appearing eerily real.

Even ghosts made of sheets flowed up above in a fan-generated breeze, making them appear even more realistic. Ghostly sounds whispered through the building, and they heard moaning nearby. Okay, she didn't think she could be spooked, but she was. What if the real ghost was upset by all the partying here?

Sheet lightning alternating with forked lightning lit up the dark greenhouse windows, the sound of rain pouring down, and thunder crashing adding to the scary atmosphere. Then a blood curdling scream made Rosalie jump half out of her skin. She was ready to remove her clothes and shift into her cougar to protect herself, despite knowing that this was just all pretend. She hoped. It was perfect.

Kolby took hold of her hand and she figured he could smell her anxiety. She bumped against him and smiled. Until a mummy came at them, startling her and she gasped. In protective mode, Kolby hurried her out of his path and past one of the garden tables. But then a zombie toddled toward them, wrapped arms outstretched to grab them, and Kolby pulled Rosalie under the table and out the other side.

Omigod, this was too great. A vampire jumped up onto one of the tables and Rosalie let out a strangled cry. The vampire grinned, showing off his menacing teeth, then said, "Such sweet blood I smell close by."

After Rosalie and Kolby were standing again, she pulled him toward the door in a rush, but another zombie came after them. The Hocus Pocus witches entered through the other door and the first zombie and mummy went after them. The ladies all screamed.

Her heart pounding, Rosalie laughed, but she and Kolby were trying to dodge the second zombie. Luckily, these zombies and the mummy moved slowly, giving the "good" guys a chance to escape the monsters. The vampire seemed to be having fun just hopping up on tables to scare all the newcomers to the haunted greenhouse.

Two more zombies appeared from under a table and Rosalie screamed again. She couldn't help it. They just startled her, and they were only inches away from her. Kolby ran her around another table to get away from the other two. It was like a different kind of maze. One to escape the monsters.

The sound of a wolf howled, and they heard moaning, and a scream, not from anyone actually in the greenhouse, but more soundtrack spookiness.

Her heart racing, she shot straight for the back door of the greenhouse and pulled it open, and then jerked Kolby out of the haunted house. He shut the door to keep any of the monsters from coming out to get them.

She started to laugh. "This has been the most fun ever. I would never have come up with such a scary haunted house. I really didn't believe I'd be scared."

He hugged her. "We had a blast making it and making the costumes. The ranch hands will talk about this forever. Well, everyone will. We'll have to go the séance in the greenhouse later."

"I look forward to it. After we eat and dance." They headed inside the mansion to enjoy the food and then after eating chicken wings, deviled eggs, and rolls—though there were a ton of other foods to eat that they could sample later—they walked into the ballroom to dance.

Disco lights were flashing all over the room, making it appear wild and spooky, and fantastical, perfect for a Halloween party.

That's when she saw Eric dancing with Avery. He appeared to be having the time of his life, smiling, carefree. Rosalie was so glad for him.

Even little kids were dancing. Everyone was having so much fun. Rosalie and Kolby kicked up their heels, or waltzed to the slow dances, even dancing to Michael Jackson's "Thriller"!

Once Rosalie and Kolby had danced to several songs, she asked him, "Do you want to learn what awaits us? We can have Nina or Ava read our fortunes." She was so hoping they might learn more about the appearance of the intruder.

"Let's do that," Kolby said, taking her hand and leading her into the meeting room where Nina was finishing up a reading for Shannon. Chase's wife smiled at them and headed out the door. It looked like Nina had good news for her.

Curly, the vampire ranch hand was next in line for a reading, and she looked up at him and he flashed his wicked vampire teeth at her.

"Okay, Curly"—Nina cast a smile in Rosalie and Kolby's direction—"you will be moving up in the world."

"I get Kolby's master bedroom at the ranch house!" Curly laughed. "But Ted already told me that. What I want to know is since Ted stayed there and ended up with a beautiful white cougar, and Kolby stayed there and found just as lovely a cougar to mate, what does my future hold?"

"I see nothing yet, but maybe in the future, I will." Ava smiled at him.

Curly shook his head and smiled at Kolby and Rosalie on the way out, showing off his fangs again.

"I never had a fortune teller tell me that I'd meet the love of my life either, but congrats on getting my bedroom." Kolby slapped him on the back as Curly headed out. "You go first for your reading," Kolby said to Rosalie.

Nina had Rosalie take a seat in front of her decorated table featuring a crystal ball, the table covered with a purple brocade cloth trimmed in gold fringe. Both she and her sister, Ava, were starting to look pregnant, both carrying twins. Neither Dr. Kate nor Dr. William knew what the gender of the babies were yet. "I know what you want to learn about," Nina said.

"The intruder, if you can see anything about him," Rosalie said.

"Let's see." Nina took Rosalie's hand and held it, then released her hand. She whispered, "He's close by."

Chill bumps crawled up Rosalie's spine. She and Kolby both looked around as if they would see him standing near the table watching them. He couldn't be. Nina would have arrested him on the spot.

"Where?" Rosalie whispered back.

"Here. Watching. Waiting. He's here."

"What does he look like? What is he wearing?"

"He's wearing a lightweight, waterproof, black jacket, black hiking boots, blue jeans, and a black shirt. His hair is dark, but I can't see his face. He...he smells like a...snow leopard."

"No." Rosalie hadn't wanted to hear what she was afraid she would hear. It had to be Eric's dad.

"Hey, I'll be your shadow," Nina said.

Rosalie took a deep breath. "But you're manning the booth."

"Ava will take over for me."

Rosalie looked at Nina's pretty, silky mauve costume. She wasn't wearing handcuffs, zip ties, or a gun. How did she think she was going to apprehend the housebreaker?

As if Nina read her mind, she said, "Don't worry. I have a way of apprehending people that doesn't require a gun or handcuffs."

"Your hands are lethal weapons," Rosalie said.

"They are. My feet are too."

"And you're carrying twins," Kolby reminded her.

"True. But we also have so many law enforcement agency types here, we've got you covered. First, though, do you want me to give you a reading, Kolby?" Nina asked.

"Yeah, and then we can go and check out the séance in the greenhouse," Kolby said.

Rosalie sure hoped they didn't cause the ghostly gardener any more trauma than she might already be experiencing from the invasion of the mummy, the vampire, and the walking dead!

~

NINA TOOK hold of Kolby's hand and frowned. "You...you plan to adopt Eric. You and Rosalie."

Rosalie looked sharply at Kolby. He smiled. "Well, I want to."

"But we have to get Eric's father's approval if we're going to do it." Rosalie smiled at Eric. "We haven't even talked about this."

"It's been uppermost on my mind," Eric said.

"Thank you." Rosalie gave him a hug and a kiss. But then she asked, "Do you see an outcome, Nina?"

Nina shook her head. "No. Just that Kolby has the paperwork, and he was filling it out." Nina waved at Ava. "Hey, sis, I need you to take my place. I'm going to watch over Rosalie, Eric, and Kolby."

"Why?" Ava sounded worried.

"I saw the intruder. He's here. Somewhere. Out of sight. Waiting for the right time to approach Rosalie or Eric, I suspect. We're going to the séance. The guys are all law enforcement, and they can be there for them."

"Are you going to call Dan?" Ava asked.

"Yeah." Nina got on her phone and called Dan to warn him that the intruder was somewhere on the premises, at least in her vision.

Then Nina, Kolby, Eric, and Rosalie went outside to the greenhouse where all the ranch hands terrorizing visitors there had settled down and waited for Chase to begin the séance with Stryker and Leyton.

Rosalie, Eric, and Kolby sat down at the table with the men and several others joined them. Even Andy, who could see ghosts, was there with his spidery ghost senses. Kolby squeezed Rosalie's hand. She shivered and squeezed his hand back.

Then Chase began the séance, and everyone was deathly quiet. "She's here," he said. "Mrs. Charity Squire. She's busy gardening, concentrating on her flowers. She's been ignoring us with all our wild Halloween hauntings."

Kolby was sure Rosalie wanted to ask a million questions. He certainly did, but he didn't think he was allowed to speak during the séance without interfering with the process.

"She passed on here. She put her hand on her heart," Chase said.

She had died of a heart attack, Kolby figured.

"Would she be upset if we garden in here?" Rosalie asked, surprising Kolby.

"She would welcome it," Leyton said, his brother agreeing.

Chase nodded. "She has waited many years to see her gardens come to life again. She...she just left."

Chase, Leyton, and Stryker took deep settling breaths. Chase smiled. "She is a good spirit and is glad someone has come to restore the mansion and her beloved greenhouse to its former glory."

"Yeah," Stryker said, "she said she loves roses. But any flower that grows here in Colorado will do."

"Red roses are her favorite." Leyton smiled. "We have a group who grow a community garden every year. I'm sure everyone would love to start seedlings early in the greenhouse and will enjoy helping you to grow other things."

"Oh, that sounds like a great idea," Rosalie said. "Maybe the kids who are homeschooling would be able to grow some plants for a science project."

"Good idea," Chase said.

Andy finally said, "She loves sunflowers too."

"Yeah," Chase agreed.

"We'll be sure and put a number of flower varieties in for her then." Rosalie sounded eager to take on another project.

Kolby was glad that everyone was including Rosalie and Eric in all the happenings in Yuma Town. But this business with the intruder? That was another story. He was sticking to Rosalie the whole night through.

"Oh, and I'm staying the night for your protection," Stryker said.

Leyton shook his head. "My brother beat me to it."

"You're just slow, old man."

"But first, we have a couple of birthdays to celebrate," Addie said. "Rosalie's and Dan's."

"Oh, wow," Rosalie said. "I'd forgotten all about it."

Dan laughed. "Addie swore we were going to have the belated birthday party for me tomorrow."

They made a mass exodus to return to the mansion and celebrate birthdays then. As soon as they walked inside, Addie and Mrs. Fitz brought out the cakes Ava had made to the smaller dining room. A big cookies and cream cake for Rosalie was shaped like a big heart, decorated with a spell caster, wand, and sparkles. It was magical. She loved it. Dan's was a chocolate mud cake—an Australian dark chocolate cake with coffee-flavored liqueur—decorated with a sheriff's badge and a cougar family of four, his four greatest loves, and some orange pumpkin candy for the Halloween theme.

Once everyone sang happy birthday to both Rosalie and Dan, they opened their presents. Addie's exquisite gift to Dan had been a beautiful guitar. He was delighted. Kolby and Eric had gotten Rosalie a brand-new computer and a laser manuscript printer for working on her stories. She couldn't have been more thrilled. Then everyone ate cake and ice cream. Most everyone ate a slice of both cakes because they just looked too good not to eat one of each.

"Hey, is everyone ready for a run?" Dan asked, once everyone was finished with their dessert.

They were all in agreement.

They began removing their clothes, shifting, and then they

all headed out the front door or the back door to run as cougars, except for Eric running as a snow leopard, and Stella also stood out in her beautiful white cougar coat.

For a while, they ran on their property and then they headed to the Havertons' ranch to run across their acreage since it was much larger, using the new entryway from the Squire's estate to the Haverton's ranch, using the walking path on either side of the cattle guard, perfect for a bunch of cougars, and a snow leopard.

They were having such a ball, playing tag, sprinting with each other to certain points, pouncing on each other on the way. Kolby was having the best time ever. He loved playing with his mate, and he relished the idea that Eric was having a ball with the teens as they tackled him and he tackled them back, everyone racing each other to try and beat one another.

When they finally finished their run, they headed home to the mansion, and everyone was shifting and dressing and getting ready to go home for the night. Kolby realized that some of the people had stayed behind and cleaned up the kitchen and left food in their fridge and took the rest. Others were taking care of young ones that had fallen asleep on napping mats in one of the meeting rooms, all tuckered out from their wild Halloween party.

The band had packed up and left. Even the spiderwebs on the chandelier were gone. Kolby chuckled when he saw that. Just one chore he wouldn't have to do.

There would be lots more work to do—moving the haystacks back to the ranch, taking down the scarecrows, removing all the spooky stuff from the greenhouse, but Chase said, "It's really late so we'll be back tomorrow. Don't you all try to tackle the rest of the cleanup on your own."

Ava's husband, Chet Kensington, also a CSF agent, said, "I'll be here first thing in the morning to help with the cleanup and

I'm staying tomorrow night, if we don't catch the intruder before then."

"Thanks, Chet," Kolby said. Everyone had been wonderful about helping to watch for the guy. But after what Nina had said, he suspected when everyone left, the man would show up.

"I've got ranching duties in the morning," Eric said, picked up the kittens from the cat room, and headed up the stairs.

Kolby smiled. Eric had been a real workaholic since Kolby began mentoring him, and he already had his own horse to take care of—courtesy of the Havertons—as a belated birthday gift, once they knew he was really eager to take care of a horse of his own and love on it. The Havertons were the greatest. Not only that, but Eric had received his first driver's license, and everyone was so proud of him.

Stryker joined them in the living room. "I'll be heading down to the basement if you need me for anything."

"Night, brother," Leyton said, and he and several others started to leave, saying their good nights to each other.

Before Ted and Stella left, she said, "You tell the intruder, if he's Eric's dad, that you have a lawyer who will fight him every step of the way if he decides he wants custody of Eric at this late date and Eric doesn't want to go with him."

"Thanks, Stella," Rosalie said, Kolby thanking her also. Once they had left, Rosalie locked the front door and the cougar door. "Thanks, Stryker, for staying the night."

"You're welcome," Stryker said, "night you two." He headed down the stairs.

"I'll get the back doors," Kolby said, and he took off for the back of the mansion.

It had been the best Halloween party ever!

When someone knocked on the front door of the mansion, Rosalie was afraid they'd locked somebody out who needed to grab some of their personal stuff from the house, like a phone, keys, or something. She opened the door and standing before her was one tall dude, no one she'd met before, wearing a jacket, boots, and shirt just like Nina had described him. He smelled like a snow leopard.

"If you're coming to take Eric back to Alaska," she blurted out, "you can't."

"I—"

"He has me, his sister—"

"You're a cougar."

"I'm his sister! He has a whole town of cougars here who love him and treat him as one of the family. He has a job and friends. He's part of the local community and you can't take that away from him."

"I—"

"Why the hell have you been sneaking into the basement of our home?" Kolby angrily asked, coming to Rosalie's aid in an instant, his cell phone out and ready to call Stryker, Rosalie figured.

"I—"

"You've taken damn long to come here to speak to Eric," Kolby said.

The man raised his hands in defense, "I—"

"Don't try to deny you're here to make Eric's life a living hell. And ours," Rosalie said.

"I don't know anything about your basement," the man said. "And"—he let out his breath—"I'm William Wright, a snow leopard, as I'm sure you've guessed. If I'd been in your basement, you would have smelled me."

"You wore hunter concealment spray," Rosalie accused. "Don't you pretend that you didn't hide what you were when you broke into our basement."

"I've...I've never been here before. I swear it. I've never been in your house, basement, or any place else on the property before tonight."

"All right, let's say we believe you," Kolby said, "it doesn't change the fact that Eric wants to stay with us."

"That's fine. I didn't come here to take him away from here. I came to tell you that his dad died. I'm sorry it's taken me so long to come with the news, but my triplet brothers and I were trying to decide who would go to tell you the news and then we had to track you down after you left Loveland. We didn't even know Mac Weber had a son until he was dying. He nearly drowned in an ice fishing accident. Before he died from pneumonia, he asked my brothers and I to find his son and tell him he was sorry. I'm just one of a few snow leopards in White Bear, Alaska. Bear shifters run most of the businesses there. But we're all friends."

"Oh," Rosalie said, and Kolby took hold of her arm and steadied her.

Eric must have heard them talking or had seen the new pickup out front from his tower window and came down to see them. "So you're my dad. I'm not going anywhere."

Kolby finally said, "Why don't we all go into the living room, and you can explain what you told us? This is William Wright, a friend of your father."

Suddenly, Stryker threw open the basement door and they thought he had heard that they were speaking to the intruder, and he came to arrest him or be their backup. But instead he said, "I found your intruder!" Then he saw William and said, "Who the hell are you?"

"A friend of Eric's dad who came from Alaska to give Eric some news," Kolby said. "Someone else is in the basement?"

Which didn't make sense that Stryker was coming upstairs without the intruder in handcuffs then. "Yeah, but not quite of this world."

"A ghost?" Rosalie asked. Oh, God, not another one. Only this one was too close for comfort.

"Yeah." Stryker frowned at William. "So what's the deal with you?"

Poor William relayed the information about Eric's dad's death again, but he said, "Listen, I know he wasn't a good dad. He never married again, never had any children, but he left everything he had to you, Eric. You were his only living relative. Also, I want to extend an invitation to all of you, not just Eric, to come and visit the snow leopards in our area anytime. We have a great shifter community with Arctic wolves, the bears, even Arctic foxes. We'd love to have you come and visit."

Eric said, "I would love that. If my sister and Kolby can come too."

"They sure can. Here's my card." William handed Eric the card.

"Hey, you can stay here with us for the night, can't he?" Eric asked, sounding thankful he didn't have to go with a father he didn't know and leave all his friends and his family behind.

"Yeah, for sure," Rosalie said, so relieved that no one was stealing her brother away from her. Then she turned to Stryker and said, "So what is a ghost doing in our basement?"

KOLBY COULDN'T BELIEVE this turn of events—that Eric's father was dead and no longer an issue as far as who would raise the boy. Kolby planned to get the paperwork filled out pronto so he and Rosalie could adopt him and then he realized that was just what Nina had envisioned.

He never expected to learn that Eric's father would leave him his properties, though Kolby was glad for it, to make up a little for not helping to support him or to be a father to him all these years. As long as Eric wanted to visit Alaska, he was all for it. He and Rosalie would go with him though. He'd never been there so he was looking forward to it.

Rosalie smiled. "Uhm, we've got some fresh sheets for one of the beds. We'll get it set up in a jiffy."

"Thanks, if it's no trouble," William said.

"Not at all."

"Uhm, I guess if we've discovered the intruder is just a ghost —" Stryker said.

"Can't you exorcise him?" Rosalie asked.

"Is he good or bad?" Eric asked.

Kolby hoped he would be okay. He was surprised the ghost hadn't appeared any of the other nights while their ghost sensitive people were staying in the basement to watch for the intruder.

"Max Squire was a woodworker, and when I picked up one of his old woodworking tools, he suddenly appeared to me. He loved to make things out of wood. He told me that he did a lot of the trim work on the mansion. Chase will have to talk to him all about it," Stryker said. "We couldn't smell him because he's a ghost."

"Unbelievable." Kolby was so ready to call it a night with Rosalie after a wild and exciting day. He looked over at Eric. "Are you all right about learning the news about your dad?"

"I didn't know him at all. So yeah. I'm just relieved I don't have to leave with him." Eric glanced at William as if he shouldn't say something like that about the dead.

William said, "We totally understand."

Stryker said again, "Since your intruder is just a ghost—"

Rosalie smiled. "Yes. You can go home. We have two snow leopards and two cougars to deal with it. Thanks for being here for us and learning the truth. Oh, how come no one else knew about him? Chase? Your brother?"

"Ghosts don't appear on any kind of a schedule."

"Aww, okay." Then Rosalie frowned. "But how did he unlock the doors that one night?"

Eric looked a little sheepish. Kolby was wondering the same thing.

"Eric?" Rosalie asked.

Eric shrugged and stuck his hands in his pockets. "I dreamt I'd been in the basement looking out at the rain that night both doors were unlocked. That's all."

"You were sleepwalking," Rosalie said, sounding surprised. "I've never known you to do that, but then again, if I hadn't been awake to witness it, and you didn't remember anything about it afterwards, that makes sense." She sighed. "Thanks, Stryker."

Kolby thanked him also.

"You're welcome. I need to let Dan and Leyton know what's going on here and that there's nothing to worry about. Good night, folks." Stryker headed out and Kolby locked the door after him.

But then Kolby got a call from Mrs. Fitz. "Hi, I called Rosalie's number, but she isn't picking up. I've got news about Eric's father."

"He's dead." Kolby explained to her about the snow leopard bringing them the news.

"Oh, wonderful, I just wanted to tell you right away about it, that you had nothing to worry about, concerning him coming to take Eric away. And tell Eric I get tons of compliments on his painting in the shop. I want to order another one."

Kolby smiled. "I sure will. And thanks for the news."

"You're so welcome. We think the world of Eric and wouldn't want to part with him. I'll let you go. Night!"

"Night, Mrs. Fitz." Kolby ended the call and said to Eric, "Mrs. Fitz has gotten so many compliments off your painting, she wants to commission another."

"Hot damn. I'll get with her tomorrow about it," Eric said. Then to Kolby's surprise, Eric said to William, "Come with me. You can pick out a room and I'll change the sheets. So tell me about Alaska."

Kolby hoped Eric would ensure William got a room far from theirs. It was Rosalie's birthday, and he wasn't ready for the night to end with her just yet.

Kolby took her hand and led her to their room. "I think Eric was kind of happy to meet one of his kind."

"I agree. What do you think about a honeymoon in Alaska?"

"And we'll take Eric with us?"

"He can stay with the snow leopards and then run with his own kind while we do our thing."

"You've got a date, Rosalie. Happy birthday, my spell casting she-cat."

"You caught me in your own spell from the moment you walked into Mrs. Fitz's shop."

"I wanted to join you in the worst way, but if I had delayed bringing the sandwiches back to the ranch any longer than I had, they would have sent the sheriff after me."

She laughed. "I love you." She began peeling his clothes off him.

"I couldn't love you any more than I do." And then he was just as eager to remove her clothes and finish what they were starting.

EPILOGUE

Ever since the Halloween party, Rosalie, Eric, and Kolby's brother had been planning a fun celebration for Kolby's birthday for November 15th. That morning, she and Eric pretended that she had forgotten all about it, though she was a little suspicious when she kissed him goodbye to go to work that he hadn't mentioned it. Eric was going in with him to work with the horses and she hoped he hadn't let it slip already about the surprise birthday party. He was so excited about it, that she was afraid he might have.

Once she called Kolby's brother, Ricky, to tell him Kolby had gone into work, it didn't take long for Ricky and his mate, Mandy, to show up to help decorate the dining room and ball-room so they could have Kolby unwrap his brand-new saddle, Stetson, and chaps at his birthday party. Ricky had driven the new Jeep into the garage to hide it. Rosalie and Mandy added a bow and streamers.

Eric was also giving Kolby the painting he'd wanted for the bunkhouse: a western theme of cowboys riding their horses, cougars running alongside them, and one snow leopard too with a backdrop of the mountains. Though now Kolby was living with Rosalie and Eric at the mansion so the painting might go in their living room instead.

Once they had decorated everything for the party, Rosalie called Hal. "It's birthday time!"

"I'll tell Kolby he's needed at home because you have some news, but I'll say you wouldn't tell me what it was about."

"Okay." Kolby might think she was pregnant, which she just learned she was after she said goodbye to him this morning, so that worked too.

"We'll be over in shifts to wish him a happy birthday," Hal said.

"We'll see you all soon." She loved how they would all make a big deal of birthdays in Yuma Town. She had never felt more special than when they celebrated her birthday and Dan's at the Halloween party. She hadn't expected it at all.

She'd barely slipped her phone into her pocket, told Ricky and Mandy that Hal was telling Kolby to go home and then the party would begin, when her phone rang. It would be an all-day affair while Yuma Town cougars dropped by to wish Kolby a happy birthday. She thought others would get here before Kolby did.

She saw the call was from Kolby and could tell it was on Bluetooth when she answered it.

Kolby asked, "What's wrong?"

She smiled. He had to know they were throwing him a birthday party. "Well, I want to tell you in person what I need to tell you."

"We're pregnant!"

She laughed. "Yes, we're pregnant."

"We are!" He sounded like the happiest big cat in the world.

Eric said, "I'm going to be an uncle? Woohoo! I get to teach them how to ride a horse. And how to paint."

She chuckled.

They had taken the new road between their properties, Kolby driving, even though Eric could now, but she knew Kolby practically wanted to fly home to check on her and didn't want Eric to get himself into trouble should he lose control of the truck.

She went outside to greet them as soon as they parked the ranch's pickup. Kolby, all smiles, exited the vehicle in a rush, Eric right behind him.

Kolby lifted her off her feet and swung her around, then kissed her. Ricky and Mandy came out to wish him a happy birthday, not expecting the news she was pregnant.

When Kolby told them, Ricky said, "Hot damn, I'm going to be an uncle."

"I'm going to be an aunt," Mandy said, giving Rosalie a hug.

Then Kolby frowned. "What are you doing—"

He didn't have a chance to finish what he was going to say as they all shouted, "Happy Birthday!"

Then everyone began arriving. Ranch hands took shifts to come and visit, to eat, hand over gifts, and wished Kolby the best. Hal, Tracey, and their children, Ted and Stella ended up there too.

The beautiful cake Ava had made of a cowboy on horseback, a dog running behind him, a cougar and snow leopard beside him was on display. Mrs. Fitz lit all the candles.

Rosalie loved how everyone included Eric in their world of cougars. He belonged with them. He was one of them. Different, but a big cat too. All the deputy sheriffs and their families, the sheriff and his family, every one of the CSF agents and their mates, the doctors, their mates, the nurses and their families, all the teens who had become Eric's friends, everyone dropped in to celebrate. And of course everyone had to love on the kittens too.

Kolby was overjoyed that Rosalie and everyone else hadn't forgotten his birthday. How could she forget such a special day?

She loved her big cat with all her heart. Moving here and mating Kolby had been the best decisions she'd made in her life.

KOLBY HAD BEEN certain that Rosalie would do something special for his birthday, but he hadn't expected it to be as grand as all this. He was having so much fun as Ted and Hal grilled steaks for everyone who was there at the time, and then they'd take a break and others took over to grill steaks for newcomers, even Eric taking a turn. The cake that Ava made was beautiful, and he swore everyone had come from Yuma Town to make his birthday special. But more special than anything? Learning that Rosalie was pregnant. That was the best birthday present she could give them.

She kissed him and Ricky opened the garage door while Mandy backed out a bright new, shiny blue Jeep.

Kolby's mouth gaped. He couldn't believe it. "For me?"

Rosalie had kept telling him they'd get him a new vehicle before Christmas. He'd been using the ranch's pickup so hadn't needed to get anything right away.

So this was the reason Rosalie had been putting him off for the last two months! He adored her.

"I love it." He kissed Rosalie soundly.

Eric was running his hand over the hood. "Nice. When do I get to drive it?"

"You've got your own, buddy. Don't mix them up and take mine for a spin by mistake."

Eric laughed.

After they ate steaks, french fries, and a mix of veggies, they had champagne, milk and juice for the kids and for all the pregnant mothers. After enjoying the birthday cake, those who were still at the mansion went running as big cats. The best conclusion of a birthday party ever.

Though that afternoon, they received even more great news —the adoption papers had just come through and Eric never had to worry about who had custody of him until he came of age.

Just around the corner was Thanksgiving and Kolby knew just what he was thankful for—new neighbors at the old mansion—which meant a mate he loved for life and a younger brother to look after who was just as wild and fun as his brother Ricky. And just as much loved.

ACKNOWLEDGMENTS

Thanks so much to Donna Fournier, Darla Taylor, and Lor Melvin for reading my book and helping it to be the best it can be. You ladies are the greatest.

AUTHOR BIO

USA Today bestselling author Terry Spear has written over a hundred paranormal and medieval Highland romances. In 2008, Heart of the Wolf was named a Publishers Weekly Best Book of the Year. She has received a PNR Top Pick, a Best Book of the Month nomination by Long and Short Reviews, numerous Night Owl Romance Top Picks, and 2 Paranormal Excellence Awards for Romantic Literature (Finalist & Honorable Mention). In 2016, Billionaire in Wolf's Clothing was an RT Book Reviews Top Pick. A retired officer of the U.S. Army Reserves, Terry also creates award-winning teddy bears that have found homes all over the world, loves to garden, create photo composites, helps out with her grandchildren, and she loves on her two Havanese dogs all the time. She lives in Spring, Texas.

ALSO BY TERRY SPEAR

Heart of the Cougar Series:

Cougar's Mate, Book 1

Call of the Cougar, Book 2

Taming the Wild Cougar, Book 3

Covert Cougar Christmas (Novella)

Double Cougar Trouble, Book 4

Cougar Undercover, Book 5

Cougar Magic, Book 6

Cougar Halloween Mischief (Novella)

Falling for the Cougar, Book 7

Catch the Cougar (A Halloween Novella)

Cougar Christmas Calamity Book 8

You Had Me at Cougar, Book 9

Saving the White Cougar, Book 10

Big Cat Magic, Book 11

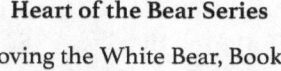

Heart of the Bear Series

Loving the White Bear, Book 1

Claiming the White Bear, Book 2

The Highlanders Series:

Novella Prequels:

His Wild Highland #1, Vexing the Highlander #2

Winning the Highlander's Heart, The Accidental Highland Hero, Highland Rake, Taming the Wild Highlander, The Highlander, Her Highland Hero, The Viking's Highland Lass, My Highlander

Other historical romances: Lady Caroline & the Egotistical Earl, A Ghost of a Chance at Love

Heart of the Wolf Series: Heart of the Wolf, Destiny of the Wolf, To Tempt the Wolf, Legend of the White Wolf, Seduced by the Wolf, Wolf Fever, Heart of the Highland Wolf, Dreaming of the Wolf, A SEAL in Wolf's Clothing, A Howl for a Highlander, A Highland Werewolf Wedding, A SEAL Wolf Christmas, Silence of the Wolf, Hero of a Highland Wolf, A Highland Wolf Christmas, A SEAL Wolf Hunting; A Silver Wolf Christmas, A SEAL Wolf in Too Deep, Alpha Wolf Need Not Apply, Billionaire in Wolf's Clothing, Between a Rock and a Hard Place, SEAL Wolf Undercover, Dreaming of a White Wolf Christmas, Flight of the White Wolf, All's Fair in Love and Wolf, A Billionaire Wolf for Christmas, SEAL Wolf Surrender (2019), Silver Town Wolf: Home for the Holidays (2019), Wolff Brothers: You Had Me at Wolf, Night of the Billionaire Wolf, Joy to the Wolves (Red Wolf), The Wolf Wore Plaid, Jingle Bell Wolf, Best of Both Wolves, While the Wolf's Away, Christmas Wolf Surprise, Wolf Takes the Lead, Wolf on the Wild Side

SEAL Wolves: To Tempt the Wolf, A SEAL in Wolf's Clothing, A SEAL Wolf Christmas, A SEAL Wolf Hunting, A SEAL Wolf in Too Deep, SEAL Wolf Undercover, SEAL Wolf Surrender (2019)

Silver Bros Wolves: Destiny of the Wolf, Wolf Fever, Dreaming of the Wolf, Silence of the Wolf, A Silver Wolf Christmas, Alpha Wolf Need Not Apply, Between a Rock and a Hard Place, All's Fair in Love and Wolf, Silver Town Wolf: Home for the Holidays

Wolff Brothers of Silver Town Wolff Brothers: You Had Me at Wolf

Arctic Wolves: Legend of the White Wolf, Dreaming of a White Wolf Christmas, Flight of the White Wolf, While the Wolf's Away

Billionaire Wolves: Billionaire in Wolf's Clothing, A Billionaire Wolf for Christmas, Night of the Billionaire Wolf

Highland Wolves: Heart of the Highland Wolf, A Howl for a Highlander, A Highland Werewolf Wedding, Hero of a Highland Wolf, A Highland Wolf Christmas, The Wolf Wore Plaid,

Red Wolf Series: Seduced by the Wolf, Joy to the Wolves, Best of Both Wolves,

Novellas: A United Shifter Force Christmas

Highland Wolves of Old: Wolf Pack (Book 1)

Heart of the Jaguar Series: Savage Hunger, Jaguar Fever, Jaguar Hunt, Jaguar Pride, A Very Jaguar Christmas, You Had Me at Jaguar

Novella: The Witch and the Jaguar

Dawn of the Jaguar

Romantic Suspense: Deadly Fortunes, In the Dead of the Night, Relative Danger, Bound by Danger

Vampire romances: Killing the Bloodlust, Deadly Liaisons, Huntress for Hire, Forbidden Love, Vampire Redemption, Primal Desire

Vampire Novellas: Vampiric Calling, The Siren's Lure, Seducing the Huntress

~

Other Romance: Exchanging Grooms, Marriage, Las Vegas Style

~

Science Fiction Romance: Galaxy Warrior

Teen/Young Adult/Fantasy Books

The World of Fae:

The Dark Fae, Book 1

The Deadly Fae, Book 2

The Winged Fae, Book 3

The Ancient Fae, Book 4

Dragon Fae, Book 5

Hawk Fae, Book 6

Phantom Fae, Book 7

Golden Fae, Book 8

Falcon Fae, Book 9

Woodland Fae, Book 10

Angel Fae, Book 11

The World of Elf:

The Shadow Elf

Darkland Elf

Blood Moon Series:

Kiss of the Vampire

The Vampire...In My Dreams

Demon Guardian Series:

The Trouble with Demons

Demon Trouble, Too

Demon Hunter

Non-Series for Now:

Ghostly Liaisons

The Beast Within

Courtly Masquerade

Deidre's Secret

The Magic of Inherian:

The Scepter of Salvation

The Mage of Monrovia

Emerald Isle of Mists